Big thanks to my sister

—Nandini Thathachari—

for designing the front cover

and reviewing this book.

CHAPTER 1

A guard walked past, eyeing the prisoner in the cage closely. She was still unconscious from when she'd been knocked out a couple hours ago. All else seemed well so he hurried back outside, casting a quick protection spell on the door to notify him whenever the door was opened. But as soon as his footsteps faded away, the prisoner's eyes flew open.

She sat up straight and took in her surroundings. She was in a large room, about double the size of an ordinary jail cell. It was dark and gray and made of stone. The prisoner was held in a cage suspended to the ceiling, about ten feet above the ground. If the guards thought that made it any different from a cage on the ground, they were wrong. That just made it harder for them to see her.

She reached to her head, pulled out a hidden hairpin, and stabbed her thumb.

She muttered a quick spell as her blood dripped onto the bonds that chained her feet to the floor of the cage. They melted away like acid and the prisoner stood up. She was grateful that the guards had only confiscated her obvious weapons like throwing knives and two swords, but they hadn't taken her blood, the key to any magician's power.

Her chains were broken, but the cage that contained her was on another level. She *could* just melt the bars like she'd melted the chains, but that seemed too easy. It would likely trigger an alarm or a trap. Then she looked down and realized her thumb was still bleeding.

"Reath Alcestis," she muttered as she smeared the blood onto her whole hand and pressed it to her chest. Almost immediately, she began to disintegrate into black dust. From the dust emerged a tiny cockroach, tiny enough to leap through the bars and escape. Soon the prisoner was free, and she shape-shifted back into human form. Now the only thing standing between her and her escape was the door, but it wouldn't be shaken for such a simple trick.

The prisoner walked over to the door. She slid her fingers across the sleek metal, thinking. An idea popped into her head. She backed up a couple steps, took a running start, and rammed her shoulder into the door as hard as she could, knowing that it was enchanted to resist against this. And obviously, it didn't work. But at least it set off the alarm.

In a matter of seconds, guards were bursting into the room, their shields and spears at the ready. Prior to this, the prisoner had hidden herself behind the door, waiting for them to open in from the outside. So while they scanned the room, searching for her, she slipped out from behind them and shut the door, recasting the protection spell so they couldn't open it from the inside.

The prisoner walked down a spiral stone staircase until she reached the bottom, then looked over the edge of the prison grounds, wondering why it didn't have a fortified wall surrounding it.

"Ha, ha," said a voice behind her. Another prison guard sauntered up behind the mage, grinning like he'd just won the lottery. But this one was different from the others. He wore gold armor instead of the usual steel. A long red cape was draped over his shoulders, and a badge was pinned to his scabbard belt. This was Chief Guard Forest.

"Weren't expecting your jail to be floating, did you?" He drew his sword and pressed the tip at the prisoner's throat. She stumbled backwards, her left foot half over the edge. One false move and she would turn into a magical pancake on the empire floor.

"Not really," she admitted, trying to sound less downright terrified than she actually was. The wind blew her ribbons off, letting her long black hair wave in the wind.

"By the way," the Chief said. "You have one and a half minutes before you fail."

"I know. And I'm about to leave. Along with your title." Forest narrowed his blue eyes, pressing the tip of his sword deeper into her neck. That's when the prisoner struck. She grabbed the sword, digging its sharp edge into her palm.

"Nogard Alcestis" she whispered, closing her eyes. Forest yanked his sword from her grasp and struck, but it was too late. The blade stopped inches from the prisoner's neck, an invisible force keeping it at bay. The prisoner opened her eyes. They were pitch black. Forest lowered his sword and staggered back. A wave of fire washed over the prisoner, and her entire body began to glow, transforming into what was the most difficult spell the prisoner knew.

Her arms extended into large scaly wings and a long tail sprouted from her lower back. Her head elongated into a snout with gleaming, wicked-looking white teeth. In a few seconds the glowing stopped and out from the fire emerged a thirty foot dragon with pitch black eyes and red-speckled black scales. It threw its head up, letting out a burst of flames. The guard, who was frozen in shock, regained his senses and pressed his entire body against the jail walls behind him.

The enormous dragon stepped forward and lowered her head to the same level as the Chief's. She inhaled and roared with all her might into his face.

He fainted. The dragon grabbed him by the leg with her talons and dove off the edge and spread her fifty foot wingspan, catching the air and gliding forward. She let out a victory flame, spraying the sky with orange fire.

"Hang on tight!" she growled. The guard was now beginning to wake up and started screaming his lungs off as the dragon spiraled towards the ground. She landed, skidding a few feet forward before stopping before a very intimidating-looking man.

He was thin but muscular with a long purple cloak pinned to his shoulders. The sign of a master. The hood of his cloak was down, letting his long, silvery blond hair fall over his shoulders. He raised an eyebrow as the prisoner dropped the Chief in front of him.

"Quite a show you put up there, Eradoa. Cutting it quite close, too." he said in a questioning tone. Eradoa imagined herself back as a human, and her body complied, melting back into a regular-sized human.

"You bet," she said, breathing heavily. "But I made it."

"With thirty seconds to spare. Congratulations, Eradoa, you have passed the test. You may now bear the title of Dark Mage."

"Thank you, Elrod." Eradoa said. "But aren't you forgetting something?"

"Oh, right." The fallen guard, who had woken up again and was clutching his head, groaning. "Chief Guard Forest, you're fired. Norenheir will take your place. You will have to be discarded, I'm afraid. Eradoa, would you like to do the honors?"

"My pleasure," she said. She held her right hand in front of Chief Forest's face, and snapped her fingers with her left. He disappeared in a flash of sparkly purple dust.

"What a mess." Elrod said in disgust.

"I'll say," Eradoa agreed, equally disgusted. "I mean, what kind of guard was he? Couldn't even stop a fourteen year old student."

"No. I mean, look at the ground. Disgusting." Elrod corrected. Eradoa looked at the ground. It was covered in remnants of the purple dust.

"I'll call someone to clean it up. Until then, you are dismissed. And once again, well done on your test." The master mage swished his hand and whispered a spell word that Eradoa didn't know. The next second, she was teleported back to the fortress.

CHAPTER 2

Eradoa's family tree was composed entirely of mages and sorcerers. In fact, her great great grandmother was married to Elrod's granduncle, making her very distantly related to the old mage. She doubted he even knew who her own mother was, let alone her great great grandmother.

Nobody, actually, knew who Eradoa's mother was except for her father, and even he wouldn't tell anyone who she was. Whenever Eradoa brought up the subject, he always cut her off, saying she left him because she opposed magic. Eradoa figured he was lying and that there was a different reason why he wouldn't talk about her. The only thing she'd managed to squeeze out of him was that her mother's name was Cleo. Not very helpful, but better than nothing. She'd finally let go of the subject when her father made it clear that he wasn't going to tell her what she wanted to know.

But then almost a year ago she'd built up enough courage to go ask him one last time. That had been the last straw. Thirteen year old Eradoa had no idea why her father got so stressed when she talked about his wife, but that day he was so angry that he picked up a dictionary and hurled it at Eradoa's head. Luckily, she'd been watching the warriors train and had learned how to anticipate an assault. A fraction of a second before the ten pound book conked her out, she ducked and watched it shatter a family portrait on the wall behind her. But when she turned back, her father was gone and the door to the house swung back and forth as if someone had left in a great hurry.

A few days later on her fourteenth birthday, Elrod came to inform Eradoa that her father had left the fortress and gone to live alone. He had come to move Eradoa to the main tower in the fortress where she could learn to fight either as a mage, an archer, a rogue, or a thief. Eradoa had wanted to be a warrior, but the lessons were full and couldn't take any more students. So Eradoa chose the mage course, like the rest of her family, where she learned all sorts of spells like the acid spell and the shapeshifting spell that she'd used in the prison escape test.

Eradoa opened her eyes and found herself laying on her bed.

She swung back and landed on her arms, kicking her legs over her head and landing on her feet. She looked out the window and realized it was bright outside. So she walked over to a row of shelves lined on the wall next to her. She reached to the top most shelf and took out a tool belt.

It had six sheaths for spare daggers on one side, four loops for potion vials on the other, and two pockets on either side that were enchanted to be able to hold as much as three elephants each. She arranged six throwing knives in the sheaths, poured a speed potion, a super strength potion, an invisibility potion, and a levitation potion into four vials and strung them through the loops.

Then she put a spellbook, a notepad, a feather, and ink in her pockets in case she needed to note down something important, like new spells, or who she needed to put on her revenge list. She didn't really have anyone on her revenge list yet, but she was sure that someone or something was going to infuriate her at some point in the day.

She didn't know why, but today seemed like an especially beautiful day after passing the mage test and killing Chief Guard Forest. Her room seemed brighter, her bookshelf organized, and there were nice thoughts in her head, for once. She walked out of her room and into another marvelous, bloody day.

. . .

She was only around three steps into the hallway when a short blonde girl came up to her in a hurry. Eradoa recognized her as Zyx, Master Elrod's secretary.

"Eradoa, I have news for you." Zyx said, her voice full of terror. "And you're not going to like it. Please don't cut off my fingers." Eradoa tilted her chin up, wondering how bad this news could be. She made a silent promise to herself that nothing could be bad enough to ruin her perfectly good day, and that she would not cut off any of Zyx's fingers.

Three minutes later, two perfectly good fingers on Zyx's right hand were laying on the floor. Eradoa was storming through the halls with a blood-covered knife in her hand. Two weeks ago, master mage Elrod, along with the other leaders, had sent twelve rogue troops to raid twelve different villages.

Not a single one succeeded. And why was that?

Heroes.

Almost four years ago they'd been defeated, but now they had regrouped and were rescuing towns and saving "poor" villagers by killing the rogues and thieves. Eradoa found herself in front of the great hall, where the Council of Leaders had meetings. She slammed the door open and marched into the Great Hall.

The Great Hall was a huge, elaborate room the size of a cathedral. It had pillars lining the walls, each one engraved with bloody scenes of past battles. Hanging from the roof was a diamond chandelier bigger than herself, holding candles that flickered with blue fire, casting a calm feeling in the room. All in all, the Great Hall looked more like a palace than a villainous fortress.

In front of Eradoa was a row of five black thrones, each hosting a separate extremely intimidating figure, the masters. Together they formed the Masters' Council.

But at the moment, Eradoa was far from intimidated.

"I know what happened," she boomed. "How?" The leaders all stared down at her, shocked at seeing someone at this time. Neroon, Eradoa's least favorite of the masters, decided to speak up. That couldn't be good. Neroon was the most abominable, stupid, moronic person Eradoa knew. He had a reputation for doing stupid things like raiding villages just to steal food, pranking high officers, and other random things. No one knew how he'd managed to get on the Masters' Council. He'd been there longer than anyone, except for maybe Elrod.

On top of that, he even *looked* stupid. He was short and fat and had shoulder-length black hair. His round glasses had red lenses and barely fit on his head. He wore a brown leather robe that looked as if it were about to tear apart, and his purple cape barely made it past his waist.

"Master Elrod sent the rogues to raid the villages." He said. "Half died. The rest came back after a hard retreat." He continued. But when Eradoa frowned even harder, he added, "We plan on sending a thirteenth troop, double the size of the rest. I will go with them. We will not take this subjugation lightly."

Neroon nodded dismissively, but Eradoa hardened her expression.

"I'll come, too." she said, trying to sound firm and determined, but it sounded more like a minnow trying to be a shark.

"No, kid. You're what? Ten? Eleven?" Neroon said, examining his fingernails. Eradoa gritted her teeth.

"Fourteen, sir."

"It doesn't matter. You are not to engage in battle until you are sixteen years of age, minimum."

"Master Neroon," Elrod interjected. "Eradoa has proven to be the fastest learner I've ever trained. She may be young, but she's—,"

"Master Elrod, I understand. But she lacks the experience of the older warriors and mages." Eradoa looked at Master Darin, the leader of the warriors, who was nodding his head in agreement.

"But—,"

"You are *dismissed*." He sat back down. Eradoa nodded with respect, but was muttering under her breath.

She exited the hall, slamming the door behind her, and returned to her room. It looked dull and gray. The bookshelf looked messy and dusty, and there was a shadow over the ceiling. What was the point of being the youngest person to graduate the mage training if she couldn't use her magic for bad causes?

She made up her mind. She didn't give a flying porkchop about what that idiot thought.

She was going to fight, whether that pea brained son of a sea slug liked it or not.

And a certain invisibility potion could help her do just that.

CHAPTER 3

Eradoa reached to her tool belt and unlatched her invisibility vial. She didn't drink it yet, but just one sip would last for two hours when she needed it. Perfect. She wrapped her fingers tightly around the vial and took off down the hallway to the automat—a big, dark purple room cluttered with people trying to kill each other—,where food was served from wormholes in the air.

After a quick bite, she exited the hall and made her way down a staircase that led to yet another humongous room.

This one was the main hall. It was smaller than the Great Hall but more elaborate. It had beautiful carvings along the pillars that lined the walls, paintings of every master that had ever served at the Council, a huge ruby chandelier, and Eradoa nodded to the fortress guards as she stepped outside.

"Hey, where are you going?" one asked.

"Oh, um, just to the arena to kill this very dangerous. . .uh. . ." she searched her tool belt for something she may have stored earlier. "Tomato. Yes. Very deadly vegetable." The skeptical guard leaned closer to inspect the vegetable and Eradoa kneed him in the face, knocking him out. The three remaining guards stared at the man, who was now crumpled on the floor at her feet. Then they looked up at Eradoa, but she was already speeding toward the military base.

In a few minutes she found herself in front of a huge door. She sipped the invisibility potion and watched her body disappear. She slipped in and found Neroon, the leader of the thieves, and Kaska, the leader of the rogues, giving orders to the soldiers standing in clusters of at least people each.

Kaska talked much more sense than Neroon. While that nincompoop was ordering his cronies to steal rubber duckies, Kaska was giving her underlings a pep talk about exactly what she would do to them if they failed. In great detail, too. Much more intimidating.

It took a half hour to get prepared. While the soldiers were loading their weapons, Eradoa was thinking of the best strategy to take down the heroes in stealth. From what she'd heard from previous reports, it didn't sound like they fought head on. They were smarter rather than stronger, and were well coordinated. In other words, they were opposite of Neroon and Kaska's troops.

It took another hour to reach the next targeted village. Now Eradoa only had about thirty minutes of her invisibility left to get what she needed, which was information to keep as a bargaining chip, and a decapitated head to show Neroon and the other leaders. She split from the raid and waited off behind a tree for the heroes to come.

Sure enough, they did. At first, things were going well. The raiders stormed into houses, returning with gold, valuables, and rubber duckies. Villagers were running around, screaming. There was an occasional splash of blood.

But not for long.

All of a sudden, one of the raiders fell to the ground, an arrow sprouting from his throat. Eradoa traced the arrow's trajectory to its source, a tall spruce tree. A blur of movement followed, and when she looked back, she saw twelve more raiders lying on the ground with arrows sticking out of their throats and chests.

Suddenly, she heard the very out of place screeching of a bird. On the battlefield, two people were battling the raiders head on. They moved with startling speed, slicing and hacking down their enemies with ease. They drew all the attention towards themselves, letting a third figure sneak up from behind. She lined the ground in front of her with small brown squares and ran away. Moments later, they exploded, blowing the limbs off of any raider within twenty feet of them. It was incredible.

When most of the raiders were either dead or injured or retreating, the heroes grouped together and took on the rest by themselves. Soon, there were only a handful left.

Eradoa had to split up the heroes somehow. If she did the math, her invisibility was going to run out any time now. She dashed out from behind the tree and trailed after two of the heroes. They had forced most of the raid into retreating, but didn't celebrate, as if this was something they did on a daily basis.

Eradoa thought of a bow and arrow and it appeared in her hands. She glanced down the line of heroes, looking for a weakness.

There.

She laid her eyes on a tall, freckled boy about her age. He had buzz-cut blonde hair and silver armor that was covered in scratches. A stream of blood trickled down one of his legs, giving him a slight limp. Perfect.

She shot an arrow, nailing him perfectly in the shoulder. It didn't seem to do much, as he easily yanked it out with a grunt, but it was enough to draw his attention.

"There's something over there." He said to a girl next to him. "Let me go check it out." He ran off with his sword clanking against his shield. Eradoa took off away from him, leading him farther into the village. She entered a large brown hut and purposely slammed the door open loudly to lead him to her.

As soon as he entered the hut, Eradoa grabbed his arm, judo flipped him over her shoulder, and pinned him to the ground. Right at that moment, she faded back into view. Perfect timing, too.

"What the—," the hero started.

"Save it," she interrupted sharply. "I want answers." She slipped a throwing knife out from her tool belt and held it against his throat.

"Who are you?" he croaked.

"That's not important." She paused and realized she hadn't asked anything yet. "Who's your leader?"

"Oh. That's it? Right. His name is Rowan. Really nice guy, best leader ever." Eradoa frowned. She picked him up and slammed him into the wall behind him.

"What are you playing at?" She asked, narrowing her eyes. He just grinned.

"Bad move," he said, grinning. "Scary, but bad."

He balled his fists and punched Eradoa square in the jaw. She fell over, her head smashing through a row of clay pots. She looked up at the hero, who's sword point was digging into her chest.

"Never let go of a high value prisoner," the hero said grimly.

"You're high value? Really?"

"I hope so,"

Eradoa tried not to look suspicious as she reached forward to the blade and put her hands up, as if she were surrendering. Then, as the hero began to let his guard down, she sliced her index finger on the blade and muttered, "Kahi Alcestis," under her breath. Before she knew it, her body began to shrink. Her toes turned into talons. Her arms turned into wings. The newly transformed hawk spread her large wings and flapped once, launching herself right at the hero's face.

She grabbed his arms with her talons and flapped her wings harder, trying to get the hero's feet off the ground. He yelled in alarm and accidentally dropped his sword while trying to slice free. Eradoa the hawk lifted him up and flew back to the fortress with the new hopefully high value captive in her custody.

CHAPTER 4

The hero cursed and yelled at Eradoa the whole way back to the fortress, making it very hard not to drop him and kill him right there. She would have, but she needed him alive as leverage against the other heroes.

At the fortress, Eradoa flew directly into the Great Hall and dropped the hero in front of the row of thrones. What was left of the rogues and thieves all stared at her disbelievingly.

Her form melted back into human shape as she dropped out of the air. She looked up and stared directly into Neroon's eyes.

"I have reason to believe that you directly disobeyed me," he said, sounding overly annoyed. Kaska's brother, Darin of the warriors, rolled his eyes.

"And I think we can all see the result of her arrogance, Neroon. There's only one of her and she's managed to do more than either of you." He said, gesturing at the hero, who was glaring daggers at Eradoa. Eradoa gave Neroon a triumphant smirk

"But—," Neroon protested.

"*Nevertheless*, Eradoa has disobeyed a leader. Even if that leader is a muttonhead, she will have to be punished." Neroon grinned, revealing all of the muck between his teeth. "Master Elrod will determine the punishment." Everyone looked at the master mage except for Eradoa, who stared at the ground. A moment later, he .

"For disobeying the Thief Leader," he began. Eradoa was holding her breath. "Eradoa will have first watch over the prisoner. Do not let him escape. First sign of trouble, you know what to do." Elrod said. Eradoa nodded, trying to look grateful, but was cursing under her breath.

For a whole hour after

"Do I have to sleep here? Do you villains ever brush your teeth? Can you turn into a phoenix? How about a manticore? How do you go to the bathroom with all those robes on? How long does it take to grow your hair that long?" Eradoa paused, collecting her thoughts, then answered.

"Yes; yes; no; no; we don't wear so many robes; and five years. Now shut up." she flicked her hand and a gag appeared over Carl's mouth. He let out a muffled sigh.

The moon was still low in the sky when Carl finally fell asleep. Thinking it may be a trick, Eradoa was on high alert, even though her eyelids felt like they weighed a ton each.

Then, an idea hit her.

She got up and peeled the gag off from around Carl's mouth. Then she laid down and closed her eyes, just to see if he would try anything.

For the first few moments, nothing happened. And then she heard a faint whispering sound.

"No, I'm not there. I'll be out in a few minutes when I'm sure the coast is clear. Yes, I know, I'm sorry. I should have been more careful, especially now that we need to locate this creepy dude." Carl mumbled. She pricked up her ears.

"Yes, what's his name? ... Arcanum, right. Yeah, yeah, I know how powerful he is. YES! This is important! I know! I'll be there in a bit. Just wait for me at the Green Gate, alright? *Thank* you."

Now this was getting serious. But she needed to live up to Carl's plan and act as dull as he thought she was.

A few seconds later, she heard the sound of a blade shearing through rope. Carl stepped down from his pole prison.

"Brainless," he muttered, then walked off.

As soon as he exited the great hall, Eradoa got up and followed him on tippy-toes, her swords drawn. Carl looked around, trying to find the exit. He ran out of the fortress and into the land around it.

Carl stopped running when he reached a large, flat savannah. Eradoa had become an ant and hitched a ride on his shoe. He came in front of a ring of trees, the Green Gates, she guessed. Eradoa had never been this far from home. She was beginning to get a little worried.

"Hello! Arella! Where are you?" Carl shouted.

"Here," said a voice from far away. A girl a little older than Eradoa stepped out from behind a tree. She had long dark hair tied in a braid that reached all the way to her waist. Her brown skin was lined with scars and gashes, as if she'd plunged head-first into a thicket of rose bushes. She was admirable in a fierce, strong way, like the kind of person you'd go to for advice before a fight. She held a shield that seemed to have been split down the middle, then bound back together, and a double-sided axe that was longer than her whole arm.

Ant Eradoa crawled up a tree, concealed herself behind a patch of leaves, then turned into a crow so she could see better.

"Where did you go?" Arella asked.

"I got abducted by this freak mage who could shape-shift and turn invisible. She's terrifying." Eradoa snuck down the tree.

"Seriously? I thought you said you could fight!" said the other girl.

"I know, it's just, melee against magic doesn't always go well."

"Ugh. Anyways, Ezra and Rowan got the locator spell right, and we're headed to the mountains. Did anyone follow you?"

"No, I came alone. Stupid mage fell asleep on her watch." Carl rolled his eyes.

"Good. We're leaving now." Arella waved her arm above her head and a blue phoenix-like creature descended from the sky. She mounted and pulled Carl aboard.

"Hey, don't I get a rest or something?"

"Nope. Selkath, up!" and they flew off. Eradoa flapped her wings and landed on the bird's tail. It was so big it didn't even notice, not even when she carefully shifted back into human form.

As the four rose higher into the sky, it also got colder. Eradoa thought she was going to freeze. Among the bird's feathers, Carl and Arella were nice and warm, but she, who was not among the bird's feathers, was left shivering. She pulled herself higher into the bird's tail feathers and tucked herself into the layers.

Eradoa looked down at the land below her. Out in the distance, she could still see the ginormous fortress, but it was as small as her thumb from here. Every once in a while she checked herself to see if any part of her was visible, but she was still cloaked.

The tips of her shoes only began to show when the four landed at the hero base camp. Carl and Arella jumped off and headed into a large tent. Eradoa turned back into human form and took a half sip of her potion and stepped inside the tent as well. Inside was a circle of the rest of the heroes she'd seen at the raid. They were all battered and bruised even though they'd won the battle the day before.

There was this one boy who looked like the boss. He wore an iron chestplate and purple cloak. He had shaggy red hair, making him look like a very casual eighteen year old wearing silver armor. He sat criss-crossed with his fists on his thighs and a warm smile planted on his face. He stared directly up at Carl's face with icy blue eyes. Though he looked friendly, Carl took sudden interest in his boots.

"Nice to see you again, Carl," the boy said. "Impressive that you got back so soon." Carl looked up, wearing a confused expression.

"Thanks, Rowan,"

"Yeah. Maybe you could teach us all to escape dark mages who are supposedly really stupid." He stood up and clapped him on the back.

Now this was getting insulting. How many times in one day did she have to hear "what a stupid mage"?

"Anyways, Carl, now that you're here, we should get going. We have no time to lose. Go help Ezra gather his tools. Arella and Aiden, start rounding up the animals. Tamsyn," he nodded at a short, light skinned girl with dark chocolate hair tied back in a ponytail. "Stay here and fold the tent once Ezra clears out. I'll pack the weapons and supplies. We have a long journey ahead of us. It won't be an easy one."

Eradoa knew exactly what Rowan was talking about.

They were about to leave, and she needed a plan.

Fast.

CHAPTER 5

Eradoa decided it would be best if she didn't have to sneak around. She waited out her invisibility potion and hid behind a tree. There, she unsheathed a throwing knife and sliced her wrist with the cold blade. She raised her arm and felt the warm blood drip onto her face.

She took a deep breath and began to chant a few lines of a spell in her spellbook. It was permanent shape-shifting, one that lasted for as long as one wanted it to. It was an incredibly difficult spell, one only the highest level students attempted back at the fortress. But for the sake of her mission, she had to try.

A searing pain spread through her body as it changed form. She snapped her fingers and a mirror appeared in her hand. She checked her reflection.

Her face had taken an entirely different form. Her once brown eyes turned hazel, her black hair elongated and turned red, her nose got sharper, and her face took on dozens of tiny freckles across her cheekbones and the bridge of her nose.

She walked out from behind the tree and used the remaining blood to create the illusion of a lioness. She fell down on her back and stirred the lioness to life.

"GAAAAH! Help!" she screamed. The heroes left in the tent came out to see an "innocent" victim being attacked by a lion.

"Hang on!" said a girl's voice that sounded like Arella's. She charged forward with a sword and dove over the lioness's back, trying to confuse it and draw its attention to her. Sadly, it didn't work. The lioness was fixated on Eradoa, and it clamped its jaws around her arm. She drew a sword with the other and tried slashing at its neck. Arella ran back and sliced through its neck. She hadn't cut it off but the wound was enough to spill blood. As soon as it fell over, Arella came and helped Eradoa up.

"Are you okay?" she asked, gesturing to her bite mark. The lion was an illusion, and so was the wound. But Eradoa pretended like it was real, wincing when she used it to get up.

"I think I am," she said, shivering. She stood up, slipping her sword back into her sheath. "Just not good at predicting the element of surprise, in which lionesses are experts."

"Follow me. I know someone who can help with that pretty impressive bite you've got there." Arella started walking back to the tent. Tamsyn stopped folding the tent. Inside was a boy who was packing up a bunch of test tubes, vials, and round bottles. He had neatly combed brown hair and thick eyebrows, making him look like he was either fifteen or thirty-five, she couldn't tell. She and Arella sat down in front of him. Arella explained what happened and motioned to Eradoa to put her arm out.

"Hmm," Ezra said to himself. He got to work, taking out a bottle of clear liquid, probably water, and pouring it on the wound. Then he pulled out a strip of cloth from nowhere and wrapped it around her arm. All the while Arella was asking her questions, all of which Eradoa had prepared for ahead of time.

"Where did you come from?" she asked.

"A kingdom on another island. I was a mage in the army, but had to flee after retreating from a war."

"How old are you?"

"Fourteen,"

"What's your name?" Right. She'd prepared for all questions except for this one.

"Cleone," she said, thinking of her mother, "but I just go by Cleo." And before she knew it, Ezra was done. She thanked him and stood up.

"Wait, one last question. Can you fight?" Arella asked.

"Yes. I am. Why else would I be part of the army?"

"Then why did you flee? A warrior never abandons a fight."

"A warrior also never disobeys the king. His last order was to run and find a place to hide. I swore to come back soon to get revenge on those blasted bandits. Anyways, I'll be on my way. I have a ride that's waiting for me at a watering hole." She walked off to the supposed watering hole, waiting for someone to act before her plan failed. Then right before Eradoa had to give up on her idea, something unexpected happened.

"Cleo! Wait!" Arella yelled. Eradoa turned around.

"What?"

"The watering hole is the other way." Well what do you know? There really was a pond somewhere.

"Right! Thanks!" Eradoa turned around and took off in the opposite direction. When she passed Arella, the girl held out her hand.

"What exactly is this ride of yours? A horse?" she asked.

"A dragon," Eradoa replied, making something up. To be quite honest, she had no idea what she was doing. Maybe she could create an illusion to catch their attention. Arella's jaw dropped. "Why do you ask?"

"Because my Blue Phoenix was getting real agitated. Only something more powerful than her could scare her. Plus, I've been seeing giant footsteps everywhere."

Eradoa's gut did a somersault.

There really was a dragon in this savannah. Now she wouldn't have to fake having one. Eradoa was in awe of her luck, but kept a straight face.

"That's my boy," she said casually. "Now I'll be on my way." She ran straight for thirty minutes until her legs cramped. When she had to stop, the watering hole was right there in front of her. With the day's final piece of luck, there was an unmistakable dragon dipping its majestic head into the pool of water. Now if she remembered correctly, there was a spell that could tame any beast, big or small. Sadly, Eradoa wasn't skilled enough for something like that . Besides, it would be cruel to use magic on such a beast like this.

So instead she calmly approached the dragon. If there was one common thing about all animals, it was that they always had a soft spot. And if there was one thing she knew about dragons, it was that their soft spot was always in a place they wouldn't be able to scratch by themselves.

As she got closer, the dragon sniffed the air and growled. It turned sideways and noticed the crouched human making her way towards it. It growled softly as she approached, but she didn't stop. Eradoa scanned its body for any signs that made it look uncomfortable, like a restless tail or wing. It began pawing the ground with its claws, and she found that its ears kept twitching. She jumped forward and grabbed the dragon's horn, swinging herself onto its neck. She reached up and scratched it behind the ears.

Instantly its massive body started to relax, as if three hundred pounds of lead had been lifted from its shoulders. Eradoa swung off its neck and landed in front of it with her hand outstretched. She patted its snout and felt vibrations shudder through her body as it purred.

When it looked like she was safe she got back onto its back and clicked her tongue. As it turned out, riding a dragon was way harder than she had let on. It was like getting a potato to dance. So she tried what Arella had on the Blue Phoenix.

"Dragon, up." and almost instantly the dragon lurched into the sky. Eradoa tugged on his horns to make him fly over the hero camp, where she saw Tamsyn pointing up at her. Two minutes later, Arella was up on her bird and following the giant red dragon in the sky. She quickly caught up to her.

"So you weren't bluffing?" she said.

"Does it look like that?" Cleo yelled in response.

"Where are you going?" Arella asked.

"I don't know! Somewhere random."

"Hey, can you land for a minute?" Cleo nodded and pulled the dragon's horns down. She jumped off and did a roll on the ground to absorb the damage.

"What is it?" she asked. Arella landed a few seconds later and walked over.

"You have a dragon. Do you not understand what a privilege it is to own one?" Cleo raised an eyebrow.

"Really? All I did was find his soft spot and give it a little itch. That's all." she said. Arella grinned.

"Did you say you have no place important to be?" she asked. Cleo nodded. "Well how would you like to ride that dragon across the world?"

This was exactly what Cleo had wanted, but she had to keep up her act.

"If it means I won't get my revenge, then I don't know." This was all part of the plan.

"Oh, don't worry about your revenge. Our mission will take care of that."

She paused. "I'm listening."

"If you agree, I'll tell you on the way."

Cleo pretended to think about that for a minute.

"Deal. But you have some explaining to do, because I have no idea what this quote unquote mission of yours is."

Arella grinned.

"Great, let's go. I'll tell Rowan," And she ran off.

Cleo was trying hard not to smirk. Now that she was one of the heroes, locating this powerful mage would be a piece of cake. Then once she got close to him, she could slice off his head and secure evil forever. And the best part?

The heroes didn't suspect a thing.

CHAPTER 6

Cleo decided to name her dragon Solfang because it matched with Selkath, the name of Arella's Blue Phoenix. His red wings practically glowed in the sunset sky. During the flight, Cleo asked Arella a few questions, hoping to squeeze some information out of her.

"Who's the Black Sword?" Cleo asked, remembering Carl muttering something like that in his sleep.

"Sorry, you kind of showed up in the middle of a very important mission. We're taking down Evil and stuffing her head in a volcano. The Black Sword is who we're taking down, so I hope you're a good fighter." Arella said, handing her a scroll in a case labeled, "Answering The Obvious Question That Every New Recruit Asks".

"Does every new recruit really ask this?" she asked.

"Yep. Tamsyn and Aiden were our newest recruits before you, and they asked the exact same question. So we decided to make things a little easier on ourselves." Cleo looked down and started reading.

Answering The Obvious Question That Every New Recruit Asks
How Did I Know?

Billions of years ago when the planet was created, everyone was born good. But soon, the people started dying off, because nothing can last without a counterpart. So evil was born, just one little ball of darkness, but it multiplied. Soon there were five, and they had enough power to take a human form. With their new, more capable bodies, they wreaked havoc across the lands. Luckily, the worse the evil gets, the harder the good works. Heroes started fighting back, and soon they drove off the evil. But the retreat was hard, and the five Sources of Evil didn't stop. They ventured deep into the earth, where magic was strongest. There, they combined all their magic into one being, the most powerful of them all. They called her the Black Sword, after the original dark ball's specialty. The Black Sword was more powerful than any hero could ever be, swinging her mighty sword and taking off all their heads. No amount of magic could bring her down. She wiped out all the good sources in the world, and when she was certain that evil was in control she went into a deep slumber, deep underground, in her birthplace. At the core, she separated into her main attributes, the five Sources. But billions of years later, good started to reform, which is the generation in which we are now. Good was rising, so the Sources began to reform into the Black Sword. The process would take years, but once they were joined, they would be unstoppable.

"But how do we—," Cleo began, but Arella cut her off and handed her yet another scroll.

The Answer To The Rest Of Your Stupid Questions
You're Very Predictable

In a faraway land, there is a cove. In that cove, there is a monster. In the belly of that monster is a bottle. In that bottle, there is a liquid. And what does this liquid do? It starts a magical fire that lights a portal. Now where is the frame to this portal? Nobody knows. Which is why you need to find the map which will lead you to the frame. Unfortunately, no one knows where this map is, so good luck. But there is one thing peculiar about this map. It always

47

lies where you'll expect it the most. To find it, you'll have to travel exactly where you think it is.

Anyways. Once you find the map, you can keep it somewhere safe and travel to the cove on the other side of the world. After killing the monster and retrieving the bottle from its belly, take out the map and look for the portal frame. Once you find the frame, pour the liquid onto the portal and it will spread to the rest of the frame edges, eventually opening the portal. Then, jump in. But proceed with caution, as something very dangerous will appear on the other side. Sadly, nobody knows what that is, either. But if you make it past the horrors of the realm, you will find yourself at the footsteps of the lair of Archmage Arcanum.

Congratulations, you have succeeded on your mission. Now all you have to do is somehow magically wake up the wizard from his eternal sleep and convince him to help you slay the Sources before your head rolls. Good luck, and prepare to fail and die a horrible death.

"Arella?" Cleo asked. "Did you write this yourself?"

"Yep," the hero said, grinning.

"Yeah this seems like something you would do."

"I wrote the end part to annoy Rowan after he made me do the laundry." Cleo turned to look at her.

"Is he a bad leader?" she asked.

"No, just really stubborn sometimes." Cleo looked back down at the scroll.

"Wait. Arella, if you wrote this, how did you know what to write?" she asked.

"Oh. Before you got here, we found an ancient library that was from two billion years ago. It was created by the spirits that lived before humans did, the same spirits that fought the Black Sword when she was still awake. We were there for a whole week, searching for this information. I barely slept."

"Whoa. How long did it take to get all this?" She asked. She was hoping that it wasn't too suspicious of a question, but she was really trying to see if Arella would let something useful slip, like the location of this library. Elrod would find a million uses for that.

"Oh, it took forever. Turns out, if you're in there for too long, the spirits possess you. They got Ezra, and we almost had to kill him to get him back."

"Oh. How much farther left to go?" she asked.

"Only a few minutes. We've reached our destination." Arella responded.

"Already?"

"Believe it or not. You're a slow reader." Her expression turned dark. "Now brace yourself. You have no idea what you're walking into."

CHAPTER 7

The thought of being so far from home made Cleo feel dizzy. It had been almost a day since she had left, and Elrod would be furious if he found out the hero and Eradoa were gone. Of course, once she returned with the heroes defeated, he would maybe, just maybe, calm down and forgive her. Maybe.

Or she could just return now with the information and send a more skilled mage to take a better cover for the mission. That would work out much better. After all, she was inexperienced and young and totally not the type for an undercover mission, especially if that expedition was with six heroes, then he would be furious. She decided to leave. That was the better option.

Now that she had made up her mind, a new problem arose. If she left now, they might suspect her, and a new recruit just conveniently walking up to their doorstep would be extremely suspicious. She would have to think of a way to make them know she was gone and wasn't coming back.

She would have to fake her death.

"Hello? Earth to Cleo." Arella said, waving her hand in front of Cleo's face. She realized that while she was thinking, she was staring directly at Arella's nose. She shook her head to snap out of it.

"Sorry," she veered her head back to the road, or the skyway, whatever.

"We're here," Arella's playful smile had vanished and she signaled to land. Cleo pulled down on Solfang's horns and he angled his wings down. He flapped a few times to absorb the weight of his landing and settled his hefty toes on the ground. Cleo looked at Arella, but the girl was staring straight at a lake in front of her and paid no attention to anything else, as if all the mischief had been sucked out of her.

A few minutes later, the others arrived behind them. Cleo and Arella were the only ones who rode sky animals, and the rest rode land creatures. Out of them all, Ezra's ride seemed the most intriguing. It was a green and yellow clouded leopard with a super long tail, about one and a half times its own body length. All the other animals, two horses, a wolf, and a lion, were tired and sore, but the leopard seemed like it could run another hundred miles. It had cold blue eyes like Rowan's, and looking into them made Cleo feel like she was going to turn to ice. As much as she hated to admit it to herself, the leopard scared her.

Rowan dismounted his lion.

"We've arrived." he announced, as if this weren't obvious. "From now on, our journey gets extremely unpredictable." Here we go again, Captain Obvious. "Be on your highest alert." He gestured toward the lake in front of them, but no one got back on their mounts.

"What now?" she asked. Nobody answered. Rowan took a glance at Ezra. He shook his head.

"If this is the right lake, it should be green in color and deadly poisonous," he said. He plucked a twig off a nearby shrub and chucked it into the water.

It went a few inches into the water and floated back up. Rowan sighed.

"Arella, fly west and look around. Cleo go south, Aiden, north, and Carl, east. All of you report back to me in an hour and don't check anything out without backup." They nodded and went off in their directions. Cleo climbed onto Solfang and took a glance at the sun. She pointed herself north and did a half turn to face south.

"Solfang, sky," she said, and he took off full speed ahead.

After flying for nearly forty five minutes, she found nothing. The closest thing to a green lake was a small pond covered in algae. She kept looking with no luck. A few minutes later, Arella flew over on Selkath.

"Cleo, I need you here. I found something." she said urgently, and without waiting, flew in the direction she came from. As a dragon, Solfang had no trouble catching up.

During the flight, Arella was too hyped to talk about anything, which gave Cleo time to think of ways to die. Maybe she could pretend to fall off Solfang and create an illusion of her splattered on the floor. Or she could wander off into some random cave and pretend to die from drowning in a flash flood. Then she could tie a note to Solfang and tell him to deliver it to Rowan. Or she could make an illusion of a huge monster at the mouth of whatever Arella had found and pretend to die fighting. That made the most sense.

Arella swooped down at the mouth of a huge cove opening near the shore of a lake. The water wasn't green, but it had no fish. There were no shrubs or bushes around it, but a few trees lay around ten feet away. Cleo stared into the giant cove entrance, thinking of a shark that could swallow them whole. The two walked in with their weapons drawn. Arella even brought out the shield strapped to her back and crouched behind it, slowly creeping forward.

"What's wrong?" Cleo asked.

"I don't know, but if this is the right place, and I bet my axe that it is, then we're in serious trouble." she responded.

"Then why won't we go get Rowan? He'll need to know about this."

"I can't call him until I see the Cove Guardian. And besides, we still have five minutes until the hour is over." A few minutes passed. Cleo tapped her foot and looked at her nonexistent wristwatch.

"I'm pretty sure that some highly intelligent monster would probably have killed us by now if this was the right place." she said. Arella siddled away from her.

"I'm keeping my swords, thank you very much." She lowered her shield and sighed. "Looks like I didn't need to raise the alarm. Let's head back." They started out the door when Cleo heard a hissing sound above her. She drew a sword and got ready for a fight, but nothing came down. She sheathed it and kept walking.

After walking for the rest of the hour, they were still going for the exit. It was dead in front of them, but the closer they got, the farther it seemed. Another minute passed.

Two minutes.

Three minutes.

Five minutes and they were still walking. It was as if each step took them backwards. Something was keeping them from leaving. Cleo stopped in her tracks. Not something.

Some*one*.

Someone with magic.

"Arella, stop," she ordered. She remembered the hissing sound she had heard earlier. If each step toward the exit had taken them in the opposite direction, then every sound she heard would come from... The truth hit her hard as a chill spread through her body.

She leaped a second too late as the Cove Guardian emerged from the ground right beneath her.

It was *huge*.

The Guardian was big and gray and ugly. It somewhat resembled a dragon, if you gave it two-foot long purple neck frills and rows and rows of revolving teeth. It didn't have any wings, but its back was lined with red-tipped white spikes, as if someone had fallen from above and gotten skewered, then ripped off.

Arella was lucky enough to not be caught by the rotating drill-like teeth of the monster. Luckily, its size slowed it down and Cleo had enough time to regain her senses before its mouth enveloped around her. She thanked the lord for Arella's quick thinking as she took hold of a long branch and tossed it to her. Cleo grabbed it and wedged it into the shark-like jaws of the beast. It wriggled around, trying to shut its mouth, but the branch wouldn't break. Cleo climbed out of its mouth and landed next to Arella.

"Thanks," she said, and made a break for the exit. Now that the monster was stuck for a while, it would be too distracted to get the branch out of its mouth than to put up its magic reversing spell again. She grabbed Arella's wrist and pulled her forward into a run.

The good news, the exit started looking closer with each step.

The bad news, the branch in the monster's mouth was beginning to crack. Cleo only had to *fake* her death, she didn't really need to die.

"Arella, tell me about the monster. Will it follow us outside?" Cleo asked.

"No, it's power is confined to the cove. If it leaves, we'll be able to crush it like a bug, and it knows that." Arella answered.

"Good. So all we need to do is step outside." At that right moment, the branch in the Guardian's mouth snapped in half and it spun around, trying to find them. The two dove behind a rock structure that was half filled with water.

Arella pulled a scroll from her satchel. It had the words: SORENOS LUMENAUREA, written in thick black ink.

"What's that?" Cleo asked.

"Spell of Shades," Arella answered. "Should protect us from detection for a few minutes, but I don't know how to use magic. I can't cast it."

"So how are we supposed to use it?"

"If we can bring it close enough to the nearest source of powerful magic, we may be able to suck it in and cast the spell by simply saying the words. Provided we don't die in the process." Cleo found this as the perfect opportunity to kill herself.

"Sounds good," she said, even though she had a feeling this was a bad idea. Trying to die and keeping Arella alive wouldn't be the easiest thing, but in the end, she found herself slinking alongside the hero and making her way directly behind the Cove Guardian. It looked hungrier than it had before.

Arella creeped up closer, Cleo right behind her. She pulled out the scroll, and, with her arm outstretched, brought it to the smooth, wet hide of the monster.

"Get ready," she mouthed. Cleo tiptoed up and got ready to pronounce the spell when she "accidentally" lost her footing, pretending to trip over a rock. She yelped, and a millisecond too late, Arella slapped her hand over Cleo's mouth. The Guardian turned around. It hissed and Cleo scrambled to her feet. Though this was all part of the plan, she was terrified.

She and Arella leaped and rolled, barely missing the beast's piercing claws as it slashed.

"I think it's been over five minutes!" Cleo screamed as they ran for the exit. But it continued to look smaller and smaller. Magic had returned to the Cove Guardian. They would have to defeat it to leave.

To buy them time, Cleo stopped and brought out three of her throwing knives. She threw one at the Guardian, who looked at the knife like it was a needle. While it was distracted, Cleo sliced her wrist open with the other knife and closed her eyes.

"Hu'ulay," she said. When she opened her eyes they were pure black. A row of seven glowing blue spears appeared in front of her. As soon as her blood touched the ground, they glowed so bright Arella covered her eyes and fell back. With the flick of a hand, Cleo sent them flying at the Guardian. Perfect. All seven spears hit their target, and the Guardian staggered back, crashing into the nearest stalagmite.

The glowing lessened and Arella stood up. She noticed Cleo standing right next to her and froze, her eyes full of fear.

She mumbled something, but couldn't seem to form words. Cleo stared at her with her black eyes. They may have looked strong and possessed, but the moment they settled back into their normal color, Cleo clutched her head and stumbled.

"Run," she said hoarsely, then collapsed from exhaustion. The last thing she knew was Arella whistling and Solfang flying in and scooping her up in his ivory talons.

CHAPTER 8

Cleo found herself laying on Selkath's feathery tail. Solfang flew above her, gently nudging her awake. She smiled weakly and patted his snout. He let out a happy puff of fire. Cleo sat up and swung herself over her dragon's sleek neck and slid down until she sat right in front of his wings. She pushed Solfang's horns forward in Arella's direction.

"Hey," she said. Arella yelped and almost fell off her bird. She settled herself back into her saddle.

"Oh, you're awake," she replied in surprise. Cleo didn't know why, but Arella couldn't seem to meet her gaze after the cave incident.

"Can't believe I'm a mage, can you?" she guessed. Arella sighed.

"Nope. I've always been a fan of magic. It's awesome and does a lot of cool stuff that I'll never be able to do."

"So why were you so stunned?"

"It's just. . .when you cast that spell, your eyes turned cold, like *you* were the one under the spell, not the spears. It was like you were in some sort of trance. Then you passed out. I have to admit I was terrified. I would have stayed there forever if Solfang hadn't come." Arella looked down at Selkath's electric blue feathers. The bird let out a comforting screech that sounded like a woodpecker drilling into a tree.

"Tell you what," she said. "You don't have to be afraid of what you control." Arella looked up.

"What do you mean?" she asked. Cleo grinned, though her next move was going to demolish her chances of defeating these people.

"I'll teach you how to use magic. Just let Rowan know we'll need all the power we can get, and he'll let us go. Come on, we've got work to do." Arella jumped off her bird and tackled Cleo in a hug.

．　．　．

Cleo had to admit she was surprised how easily Rowan let them train after their discovery of the Cove Guardian. She was also surprised by why she had agreed to make the heroes more dangerous than they already were by teaching them to use magic. These were her enemies, yet every time she saw Arella she felt less and less like Eradoa and more and more like Cleo.

But she had to hold herself together and carry out the plan. She guided Selkath towards an open plain only about a ten minute's flight from Rowan and the others. There were very few trees or bushes to accidentally set on fire and moist savannah grass lay everywhere, making it a perfect place where a few spells gone wrong wouldn't hurt the environment. Again, Cleo didn't know why she cared so much about what happened. She was supposed to help the Black Sword burn the continent to the ground. Why did she care about this worthless lump of land?

"So, what's first?" Arella asked, her eyes wild with excitement.

"We'll start with the most basic spell, a gentle breeze." Cleo said, strolling to the left side of Arella. She lifted her arms until one was higher than the other and whispered the word: "Hespero".

She didn't need blood magic to cast such a simple spell. As soon as she pronounced the last syllable of the word, she felt heavy air rolling up her arms. When they reached her palms, she curled in her fingers and thrust out her arms. A gust of wind erupted from her palms, and she realized she'd thrust a little too hard. The leaves were blown off the nearest bushes. So much for trying to preserve the environment.

Arella was quick to give it a try. She said the exact same word did the exact same motion, but forgot to curl in her fingers. The wind came gushing backwards into her face. Cleo almost fell over laughing.

Arella tried again, this time getting it right.

"I got it! What's next?" She said, giddy with excitement. Cleo was amazed with her progress already.

"Um, how about an invisibility spell?" she offered. Arella threw her head up and down, in what appeared to be a very violent nod.

"Okay. This one is less of a spell. It's a potion that you'll need to brew." She reached into her tool belt and pulled out her spellbook, ignoring the surprise on Arella's face. She flipped to a page somewhere in the middle, a page titled, 'Potions.'

"Aha. Invisibility potion." She read it over, closed the book, and slipped it back into her pocket. "We'll need fresh water, pine bark, violet oleander, and drake scales."

"Violet oleander?" Arella asked.

"Yeah. It looks exactly like the common yellow variant, just a different color. Also has medicinal properties."

"Oh! Ezra might have some." Arella said. "I'll go see if he has any."

"Perfect. While you're there, see if you can get one of Solfang's scales while you're at it."

In a few minutes, Arella was back, holding a beautiful five-petaled purple flower in one hand and a shiny red scale in the other. Cleo had scraped some pine bark off the nearest tree and conjured ice to use as water.

She waved her hand, and a tiny cauldron appeared in front of them. She mushed together the bark, water, the scale, and the purple flower and made the cauldron float. Under the pot, she set a few leaves and twigs on fire to complete the last steps of the process.

"While this boils, let's move on to the next spell. One I think you'll really enjoy."

"Like I aren't already!"

Cleo took a deep breath, wondering whether she should do this. It put her whole plan in jeopardy. She waved the thought aside and carried on.

She closed her eyes and slipped one of her throwing knives out of the sheaths on her tool belt. She sliced her wrist open and muttered, "Ser Alcestis." She melted into a puddle of black goop. Out from the goop emerged a six and a half foot tall sleek black horse.

Arella shrieked.

"You can shape-shift?"

"Yes, I can shape-shift."

"Oh my god that's crazy! When can I—, "She cut herself off all of a sudden, eyes widening as if she'd just remembered something important. "Wait, didn't Carl say he met a mage who could turn invisible and, and shapeshift?"

Cleo tried to keep a straight face, but was killing herself on the inside. How could she have been so careless?

"And is that blood magic?" She looked down at Cleo's bleeding wrist.

"Arella, I can—," Cleo started.

"Were you the one who—who, um, you know." Her eyes were full of shock and disbelief. Cleo sighed.

"Yeah. I was. But, I was only following orders. I'm sure you can understand that. Right?"

"So you worked for the very people me and Rowan and the others have been fighting for years?"

Cleo hesitated, then answered, "Yes," she was done lying.

Arella was silent for a long moment. Finally, she said, "Ok."

"Huh?" Cleo said. "You're not mad?"

"Yes, I'm mad, but I know you're on our side now. Otherwise you wouldn't be helping me."

"But—,"

"Bruh. You really thought I would be crazy mad at you and take revenge, didn't you? Oh man, that's hilarious. I—," she opened her mouth to continue but what came out were just more laughs. They were so genuine that Cleo's mouth tingled, then she smiled. Before she knew it, both of them were on the floor, giggling like psychopaths. Cleo didn't even know why. Five minutes later, they were still laughing. Arella stopped and the two got up.

"What happened?" Cleo asked.

"Look, girl. I'm not judgemental. You're helping us now, aren't you? I mean, as long as Carl forgives you, I don't care." Arella assured. Cleo let out a huge sigh of relief.

"But how do you know that I'm not a decoy or a spy or a—whatever I might be," Cleo asked.

"If you were, I can't think of one good reason why you'd be teaching me all this. No problemo."

A new feeling spread through her veins. If she continued her mission, she would kill the great mage Arcanum and secure evil forever. She'd be a legend. She might even get Neroon to admit that.

But then...what would happen after that? The Sources of evil would turn the world into a rotten wasteland of carnage all over again. And she'd have to *live* in that rotten wasteland of carnage, reminding herself every single day that it was *her fault* the world was like this.

Forget the mission. Her life was a lie.

Besides, just a day with Arella and the other heroes had completely changed her, more than she was willing to admit. If she'd lied to one of her comrades back at the fortress, they would have reported her to master Elrod and she would be executed, even if she really *had* turned to their side.

But now she needed to stop thinking about this. It was time to teach this girl everything she knew so she could so they could blast this Black Sword to smithereens.

CHAPTER 9

Cleo was impressed with Arella's speed. In just an hour, she was ready for something more dangerous.

"Ooh! What are you gonna throw at me? A tiger? A crocodile? Oh! A dragon?"

"Neither," Cleo replied calmly. "You're gonna make your own enemy. Create an illusion of anything you want to fight. You'll have five minutes to defeat it before you move on." Arella's eyebrows raised an inch and she took a deep breath to calm down.

She closed her eyes. When she opened them, a beast with a tiger's body, a lion's head, a scorpion's tail, and dragon wings flashed in front of her, raising its tail menacingly.

"Nice," Cleo said, impressed.

"Two years ago I ran into one of these while scouting. It nearly killed me."

The manticore pounced. She watched as Arella thrust her hands out, sending a gust of wind pushing the beast back. She punched the air, blasting flames from her fists. She stepped forward, took a deep breath in, and pointed four fingers at the manticore. Fire spurted from her fingers with the same force as a flamethrower. It was only a few seconds before the manticore disintegrated.

"Seriously?" Arella said in disgust. "I almost got eaten by one of these! How are they so weak!" Cleo nodded.

"Magic does that to you. It makes your previous fears seem childish." she stated. She walked forward and got ready to summon a more difficult opponent when a roar filled the air. Both Cleo and Arella turned their heads to see what had happened.

"What was that?" Arella asked. "It sounded like the Cove Guardian."

In the next moment, Aiden and his horse ran to them. There was a mix of urgency, shock and worry in his eyes.

"Poison. Bite. Ouch. Pain. Death. Help! Come quick!" Aiden said in a hurry, then dashed off, not waiting for them to follow. Cleo and Arella mounted Solfang and sped after him.

In a few minutes, they reached the Cove. Rowan was lying on the floor, shivering. His teeth clattered and his fingers trembled. His whole face was red. Arella jumped off and ran to his side.

"What happened?" she asked. Aiden hung his head.

"The Cove Guardian bit him," he knelt down and took off Rowan's chestplate, which Cleo noticed had a giant hole in the middle. Underneath was a mess of blood and torn flesh. A small chunk of his side had been bitten off, but all in all it was nothing that wouldn't heal eventually.

"What's so bad about it? I'm sure he's been in worse situations." Cleo asked, dismounting her dragon. Aiden looked up.

"It would be alright, but the bite is poisonous. In three days, the Guardian's venom will spread throughout his entire body and he'll. . .you know." he said. Cleo's shoulders sank.

"Won't magic do the trick?" she asked. Aiden shook his head.

"I asked Ezra about it. He said the Cove Guardian's poison repels most spells. No amount of traditional healing or even magic will fix this. There's only one cure. And I think we all know what that is." He let the quote hang in the air. When everyone shrugged, he sighed.

"Seriously? Nobody?" still nothing. "The tusk of the Elephant of Doom. Said to be able to cure any disease or wound when ground to dust and inhaled." Cleo lifted her shoulders up again.

"I think I know about that. But is it seriously called the Elephant of Doom?" she said.

"Well, yeah. It's a giant elephant that brings you to your doom. Pretty straightforward. But I know, not very creative." Aiden shrugged.

"Oh. And I heard it's massive and can kill you by merely stepping on you." Cleo said. Aiden and Ezra nodded simultaneously.

"Anyways, its tusks are so big, and we won't need much, so no need to harm it in any way. And definitely no need to dislodge its whole tusk." Aiden said, and the team nodded in agreement.

"There's no time to lose," Carl said. Cleo had forgotten he was there, yet looking at him gave her a weird tugging in her stomach. There was a big clump of guilt she couldn't get rid of since she'd decided to stay good a few hours earlier.

"Everyone climb aboard," Arella said, gesturing to Selkath. "We'll need to fly to move fast enough. Leave the animals here to guard Rowan." Nobody argued. They all ran to mount Selkath.

"Wait," Cleo said. "It'll be too much for Selkath to carry all four of you. Two of you should mount Solfang. He's stronger." Carl and Aiden shrugged and walked over to the dragon, when Carl stopped.

"Sorry, but that thing freaks me out." He said, shrinking down. Ezra shot to his feet and strode over. Cleo let out a silent breath of relief that she wouldn't have to be anywhere near Carl.

"I'll go. You stay with Arella." Ezra said, and happily slung himself over the dragon's sleek body. He let down a hand and pulled Aiden aboard, and Cleo sat in front of both of them.

"Hang on tight," She said, then took off.

CHAPTER 10

"So do you even know where to find this elephant?" Cleo asked Ezra as they flew.

"Yeah, it prefers greener areas, especially spruce or redwood forests."

"So where's the closest forest?" she asked. Ezra pulled a map from somewhere in his pockets and pouches.

"Here." He said, pointing at a place west of them. "Hargrove Forest."

Cleo veered Solfang to the left. "How long?" she asked. Ezra thought for a minute.

"A few hours, I think." He said. Cleo groaned. The sun was already setting.

A few hours later . . .

Starwood Forest was *huge.* It was nighttime by the time they reached it, and it took another full two hours to search the whole thing. You'd think a fifty foot tall elephant would be easy to spot.

"It's not here," Cleo said. "This must be the wrong forest. Are there any others?" She signaled Arella to bring Selkath closer as Ezra searched his map

"Yeah. But it's another hour's flight due north."

"Never mind that." She waved her hand, gesturing to Arella to follow.

One hour later . . .

The next forest seemed to be even bigger. The sun was rising by the time they'd finished searching.

"Not in my half," Arella said when they regrouped. She and Cleo had split up and each taken roughly half the forest to search on account of it being so large.

"Same," Cleo said. "On to the next, then."

The flight to the next forest was long. There were many small patches of trees and overgrowth they had to individually search every single one of them, adding an hour to their flight.

The next forest was a redwood forest, very appropriately named "Redwood Forest." It was small, and only took about five seconds to look over and come to the conclusion that it did not conceal a giant elephant.

"Is this it?" Aiden asked Ezra as his frown deepened.

"No," Ezra said, "but I wish it was. Look." He flipped the map around to show Cleo and Aiden. Cleo's heart almost jumped out of her chest.

The next forest was right next to the fortress.

"Don't worry, the forest is at its back. They won't be able to see us unless someone's patrolling." She said, then realized her mistake.

"How do you know that?" Aiden asked.

"Oh, um, me and Solfang have flown past that before." She made up.

"This is the last location on the map." Ezra said once they got there. "Elderbloom Woods." Selkath slowed to a stop behind them.

"That means if the elephant isn't here, Rowan's gonna die." Arella said. Cleo nodded, hoping with all her might that the elephant was real and it was here. The trees were farther apart, so the search should be easier here.

Turns out, it was.

The elephant was easy to spot. Being fifty feet tall, it stood out in the forest like a cat in a litter of foxes. It walked along, merrily minding its own business, munching on whatever trees were tall enough to reach its mouth. It seemed as though its tusks were longer than its tail, which swished around, knocking over the occasional tree. The tusks were around twenty feet long and five feet thick. Cleo drew one of her swords and stood up on Solfang, bending her knees slightly to stay balanced. Ezra scooted back.

"What are you doing?" he asked. She didn't answer.

"Solfang, down," she commanded, gently tugging downwards on his horns. Solfang swooped down until he was only a short distance from the elephant's eyes. Cleo jumped down and landed on the elephant's head as gently as she could.

Then, while the elephant was munching on a tree, she slid down to the base of the elephant's tusk and knelt. She brought the edge of her sword to the tusk and sheared off a piece. She waved it in the air to show the others. Then she ran to the tip of the tusk, whistled, and jumped off. A few moments later, Solfang caught her in midair. She slumped onto his back.

"That was impressive," Aiden said. Cleo held up the tusk shaving triumphantly.

.   .   .

In four hours they were back at the Cove entrance, where they had left Rowan. He was still shivering. Even worse, it was already midday on the second day. If this didn't work, Rowan would be dead by tomorrow.

"What next?" Arella asked. Ezra slid off Solfang's back and patted him. The dragon purred in content.

"Next we grind it to dust. But be careful; because—," Cleo didn't wait for him to finish his sentence. She dashed off and returned with a large slab of stone and a heavy rock. She brought the rock above her head and smashed it against the tusk shaving. Immediately a shudder rolled through her body. She dropped the rock with a yelp.

"Don't say I didn't warn you," Ezra said, sighing. "I was trying to say that the tusk of the Elephant of Doom is practically indestructible."

"Then how was I able to get this part off?" Cleo asked. She had no idea how that made any sense.

"Because your swords are sharp. That rock is not."

"Then can we keep shaving off the edges until we have dust?" Carl suggested. Cleo shook her head.

"That would take too long. We only have a day until Rowan dies." she said. The others nodded in agreement.

"Then what do we do?" Aiden said. Nobody answered. Ezra sighed, again, and stepped up.

"There is one solution," he said, and everyone's ears pricked up. "We'll have to go back to the elephant for it. Cleo, you're obviously the one for the job after that stunt you just did." Cleo smiled and drew a sword.

"You won't be needing that," Ezra said, and she frowned and slipped it back into its sheath. Ezra explained the plan and handed her a large stone that weighed at least fifteen pounds, heavier than the one Cleo had tried to use earlier. Cleo had no idea how he just found it lying on the ground. "Be careful, the elephant won't like it if you stay on its trunk for too long."

．　．　．

Cleo suggested that only she and Ezra should go this time, but Arella insisted on coming as backup.

In around ten minutes they found the Elephant of Doom. It was only maybe a half mile from where it was last time, but it was still happily munching leaves everywhere it went. Cleo would hate to disturb it, but for Rowan, she had to. She got ready to jump when Ezra tapped her back.

"Take this," he said, handing her a large buffalo skin pouch. She took it and jumped off, landing on the elephant's head. This time, instead of minding its own business, the elephant grunted in discomfort and shook its head a little. Cleo gulped and walked onto its tusk, which started to really annoy it.

This was where the hard part was.

If she ran, the elephant would shake her off. Solfang could catch her, but it was more likely that she was going to plummet to the ground and get trampled by the elephant.

But if she walked slowly, her footsteps would annoy the elephant into shaking her off as well, which would be a no go.

Either way, she was probably gonna get shaken off, so she needed a better strategy. Who said she needed to walk?

"Alcestis Skirenar," Cleo melted down into a puddle of goop that solidified into a reticulated python. She wound her twenty foot body around the tusk and slithered to the tip of the elephant's tusk. She could almost feel the elephant relaxing after it thought she was gone.

When she reached the tip of the tusk—the weakest part—, she turned back into a human and took out the heavy stone.

Cleo gathered her courage and struck the stone to the tusk. The elephant roared. Particles fell like saw dust and she caught them in the pouch. She was surprised to see how much was already filled. She struck it again and more of the pouch was filled.

In a few minutes the entire pouch was full, but the elephant was fed up. The moment she tied the pouch shut, it swung its big head and shook her off. She plunged to the ground. She had only a few seconds before she hit the ground, so she yelled the most basic wind spell, the first she had ever used. Unfortunately, casting spells while falling to your death didn't always go right. Her palms stayed warm and no wind came out.

When she hit the ground, she made the mistake of trying to land on her feet. Her feet didn't like that. A wave of pain spread through her legs and she collapsed.

Stupid broken foot. She yelled in her mind. But she had bigger problems. The elephant was eyeing her angrily. Its heavy feet were only a few yards from squashing her into a red haired omelet.

She held up a hand to signal for help. A nanosecond before she was trampled, a rough hand caught hold of hers and pulled her aboard her dragon.

"Really cutting it close there," she said to Aiden.

"Sorry. At least I beat Arella, right?" he replied. Cleo sighed.

.   .   .

It was late into the night when they were back at the Cove entrance, and Cleo swung off Solfang like she usually would. But she had forgotten she broke her right foot. Almost immediately she fell back down. She took off her boot and saw an ugly, purple bruise. Her attempt to walk had torn open a patch of tender skin near her heel. In all her panic, she'd forgotten how much her foot actually hurt.

"You okay?" Arella asked. Cleo looked up at her.

"Yeah, I just got thrown off a giant elephant, broke my foot, and almost got trampled. Never better." she grumbled. Ezra jumped down and took the pouch from her. He opened it and brought it to Rowan,

Moment of truth.

But right before he could put it under Rowan's nose, Tamsyn shared the bad news.

"Ezra, don't bother," she looked as though she had been crying. "He's not breathing anymore.

CHAPTER 11

Arella screamed.

"What?"

"Tamsyn, he's still alive," Ezra said. Arella looked as though the weight of the world had been lifted from her shoulders. "Just give him a moment, he'll start breathing again."

"But by the looks of it, we don't have that much time. Even if he starts breathing soon, we'll need to hurry." Arella didn't wait. She grabbed the pouch from Ezra and held it under Rowan's nose. Nothing happened.

"Right. We need to wait for him to start breathing." she remembered. "What do we do until then?" Cleo held up a hand.

"Ahem," she said. Arella turned around.

"Oh, right." she paused. "Um, how do we heal that? We need the whole pouch of dust for Rowan."

"We could go back to the elephant and get more," Carl suggested.

"No," Aiden started. "Because the only one of us with the guts to ride that monster is sitting over there with a broken foot." He pointed at Cleo and she grinned sheepishly.

"Also going back to that beast for a third time would be a death wish. Cleo broke her foot and almost got stepped on. Who knows what'll happen if that thing gets angrier." Ezra concluded. Nobody argued. Cleo felt like a dunce just helplessly sitting next to her dragon, not able to do anything.

"How about we take turns telling jokes?" Carl suggested. "Why did the chicken cross the road?"

"To get to the other side."

"Correct, great. Next one, why did the scarecrow—," he was interrupted by the sound of heavy breathing.

"Hhhhhh hhhhhh," it was Rowan. He was breathing again, saving them all from more cheesy Carl jokes. Apparently Cleo was the only one who had heard it. She rushed to her feet, yelped, then fell back down.

"Geez, girl. What's the hurry?" Arella asked. Cleo pointed at Rowan.

"He's awake," she said. Arella forgot all about Cleo and picked up the pouch, running to her leader. She brought it to his face and he inhaled.

"Hhhhhh. . .ACHOO!" Rowan's eyes flew open. He immediately got up and started running around, screaming. "Help! Fire! Owie! Waffles! ****! ***** ****! Aaaaaah!" Cleo raised an eyebrow.

"Is that supposed to happen?" she took a glance at Ezra, who was equally bewildered.

In three minutes, everything settled down. Rowan explained that when he inhaled the dust, it felt like his head was on fire and his saliva tasted like waffles. That was enough to wake him up.

"We need to get back in there and kill that Guardian soon. When I was out, I had a vision. I saw three people around a table. They looked like they were plotting something. Something about the mage

Eradoa going missing after Carl escaped. They're planning on looking for her, hoping that finding her will help them find us." Cleo gulped. Arella gave her a meaningful glance.

"What do you mean?" Cleo asked.

"I mean that this Eradoa mage plays an important role in whatever they're planning." Cleo gulped. The Eradoa part of her would have been worried for herself, her original plan, and her pride—if Neroon found out.

"Cleo, can I talk to you for a moment?" Arella asked.

"Sure," she said, and they stepped out, Arella helping Cleo move.

"Alright. You need to tell Rowan and the others right now." Arella ordered.

"What? Why?"

"Because you can't keep this secret forever! You think you can just play along as Cleo for the rest of your life knowing that I know who you really are and can tell them at any moment?"

"You're gonna tell them?"

"No! First of all, I don't have the guts to talk to Rowan about this. And second of all, it's *your* secret. I can't take the hit of their reactions for you." Arella replied. Cleo sighed.

"But—fine. Just, let me do it in my own time. I need to clear their thoughts about me being important and all first."

"About that, do you have any idea what they're talking about?" Arella asked.

"Who? The masters? By Rowan's description, it's most likely Elrod, Kaska, and her brother Darin. The most experienced, powerful, and dangerous. I know Elrod personally, but I can't imagine why he'd call the other two to talk about me. He usually works alone." Arella narrowed her eyes.

"Are you lying to me?" she asked suspiciously, tightening her jaw muscles. Cleo threw her hands up.

"No! I swear I'm not lying. I really don't know what they're doing." She said. Arella relaxed her jaw.

"Okay. We'll figure it out. For now, Let's head back."

Cleo nodded and they made their way back to the Cove entrance.

"How long are we gonna stay in front of this hole?" Rowan asked.

"For as long as it takes for Cleo's foot to heal." Ezra replied.

"Wait, what?" Rowan was clearly surprised.

"Long story," Ezra said. Rowan sat back down.

"No worries," Cleo said. She would tell the others about Eradoa in her own time. "You forgot I'm a mage." She waved her hand over her foot and the blood and bruises vanished.

"Wow," Arella whispered. "You've got to teach me how to do that."

"Oh, it's not healed yet. Give me a few minutes and we'll be good to go." Cleo said.

"You seriously couldn't have done this an hour ago?" Aiden scoffed. Cleo shrugged.

"I didn't have enough energy earlier." It was only half true, since she could have used blood magic, but of course, she didn't say that out loud.

A few minutes later, Cleo was on her feet and getting ready.

"Are you sure you don't have some magic armor equipping spell? It could've saved all of us some time." Aiden joked. Cleo laughed and shook her head.

Rowan handed her their spare set of armor.

"Here," he said. "Just in case we have to fight." She thanked him and asked Arella for help putting it on. Sadly, the armor was a spare, so someone had taken the helmet. It was also a little loose, but that would give her some freedom of movement, so it was okay.

She strapped up her shin guards and tied up her long red hair, getting ready for their fight with the Cove Guardian. With only Arella, she'd survived by the skin of her teeth. With five others, let's see just how long she would last.

CHAPTER 12

Cleo would like to say that she charged fearlessly into battle and took down the Cove Guardian without a scratch.

Sadly, that kind of stuff never happened to her.

Instead, she was deathly afraid and could almost feel her fingers trembling on her swords. The Guardian was incredibly powerful, and they had to defeat it to break the mirroring spell and leave the Cove. She doubted it would be tricked again.

She was about to lower her guard when she heard the same noise she had earlier. Instinctively, she looked to the direction of the sound, up. But now she knew where the monster really was.

"Dive!" she yelled, right before the Guardian erupted from the ground. She dove to the left and slashed the monster's underbelly. The blade bounced right off.

What? She rolled to break her fall and stood back up, ready for another hit. Again, it did nothing. She needed a different approach. And she wasn't planning on using blood magic any time soon.

Meanwhile, the rest of the group was doing the same thing. Trying to find the Guardian's weak spot. It *had* to have one. They kept slashing at the beast with their swords and daggers and axes. No luck.

Cleo veered around and ran straight toward the Guardian. She used her momentum to launch herself onto the monster. It roared, sending a wave of fear down Cleo's spine.

"Cleo! What are you doing?" Rowan yelled.

"Trust me!" she shouted back. She grabbed hold of the two mustache-like strands that came from the Guardian's cheeks like whiskers and wrapped them around her hands. It roared again, throwing her off. But she managed to keep her hold of the mustache, dangling from its neck like a maniac.

"I will never understand how you have the guts to do anything like this!" Aiden yelled from below. He and the others were still slashing at the monster.

And then Carl hit a spot that the Guardian didn't like. Right at the base of its tail. The sensitive spot for most creatures. A *very* hard spot to hit. She was sure Carl hit it purely by accident, but the Guardian was distracted for a few seconds.

The next moment it snapped back to reality and lashed its tail out in Carl's direction, sending him flying. He smashed through a rock column and splattered against another.

"Carl!" Aiden screamed. He ran to help his friend, but Ezra stopped him.

"Go to him later. We need you here." Aiden's expression turned hard, but he nodded. He raised his axe and chucked it at the Guardian's eyes. It blinked right as the blade was about to hit its eye, deflecting the weapon like it was nothing.

But then, if it was so strong, why did it need to protect its eyes?

Another weakness. So she could either get to its eyes or its tail. Which would be easier? The eyes, of course. She yanked the whiskers back and drove it backwards. The monster roared and threw its head back, crashing into a rock structure. It took all of Cleo's strength to keep her grip. Shards of rock shot into her skin like miniature needles. Most bounced off, but some dug into her flesh.

Feeling hardly any pain because of the adrenaline pulsing through her veins, focused her attention solely on the Guardian. She pulled the whiskers into another rock and covered her eyes for protection against another pebble rainstorm. Another crash and the Guardian was left woozy.

This was her chance. She took out one of her swords and pulled herself up the Guardian's neck, closer to its face. She nodded at Rowan, who understood. He kept the monster busy by slashing at its tail. It would be nearly impossible to hit it again, as it had the instinct to protect its weak spots, especially after the first attack. But it was dizzy after smashing through three stalagmites, which gave them an advantage.

The Cove Guardian slammed its tail into Rowan's chest, sending him sprawling backwards. Rowan lifted his axe and threw it at the Cove Guardian's tail. It swatted it aside with ease, but that was enough to keep it distracted for a moment.

Cleo lifted her sword and drove it into one of the eyes.

The Guardian let out a bone-chilling roar and yanked its whiskers out of her hands. It thrashed around like a wild horse and threw her off. She flew through the air and hit a stalagmite with a sickening *crack.* Her vision went black for a few moments, then she was up again. Arella was running to her.

"You seriously have to stop killing yourself like that!" She yelled and helped Cleo to her feet. They stared at the Guardian, who was still semi-blindly thrashing around with blood pouring from its punctured eye. Cleo's sword was lying on the ground right beneath it.

"We need to get to its other eye!" Cleo yelled over the roaring. Arella nodded.

"But you're in no condition to—," she began, but Cleo didn't wait to hear the rest of it. She took off, ignoring the burning pain in her chest. With the Guardian distracted, she took the opportunity to grab one of its waving whiskers. She yelled at the nearest hero to her, Ezra. He grabbed the other one and they both pulled down as hard as they could. The Guardian lowered its head, pulled by its mustache. Rowan ran up its tail to its head. He flattened himself onto its smooth skin and held on tight as the Guardian pulled free from Cleo and Ezra.

As soon as the mustache slipped through their hands the Guardian began to chomp its teeth and thrash around more. All Cleo could do was shout at everyone to hide. The Guardian, in its bloodthirsty stage, would easily overpower the six unlucky heroes.

Rowan grabbed its whiskers as it tried to dive for them and pulled it back right before its rotating teeth crashed into Cleo and the others and chewed them into spinach hero salad.

But the monster dove at them again, and this time it resisted the tug of its whiskers. Rowan was chucked off. Tamsyn and Carl caught him, but the Cove Guardian wasn't done. It may have been half-blind, but it knew exactly where they were. It roared and brought its drill-teeth down on them.

Cleo had a millisecond to think, so she screamed a spell in panic and brought a giant glowing shield in front of her and the others, who were staggering back like cornered lions. The Guardian bounced off the shield like a ball without a scratch on the heroes. However, the impact on the spell left Cleo exhausted. She collapsed to her hands and knees, exhaling hurricanes. The spell faded away.

The others tried to help her, but the Guardian rushed back at them.

Thinking she was dead, it lunged over her. With one final move, she brought out a sword and swiped it across the Guardian's tail as it flew over her. It thundered a roar that shook the Cove.

She stood up and dropped her sword, turning around just in time to see Ezra thrust his sword into the Cove Guardian's other eye. Right before it clamped its teeth over everyone it fell to the ground, dead. Cleo felt the weight of the Guardian's reversing spell fade. She made her way to the others and stumbled over the dead Guardian's tail.

"We did it," she said. "Now let's get that bottle and get out of here."

CHAPTER 13

After the Guardian was defeated, its skin grew softer, as if it had been wearing armor that had magically disappeared. Rowan was able to easily slash its belly and retrieve the bottle of liquid. But of course, he got a handful of blood from sticking his arm into the belly of a dead beast.

While he and Ezra and Tamsyn cleaned up and secured the bottle, Arella, Cleo, and Aiden treated Carl's wounds. He had been battered up pretty badly, worse than Cleo was after she'd been smashed against the stalagmite. He had broken his wrist, cracked a few rib bones, and fractured three of his toes. Cleo got ready with a healing spell. Unfortunately, she wasn't a skilled enough mage to be able to snap the injuries away.

"I can cast a spell on your ribs and toes, since that's not too bad. Your wrist is pretty bent and broken, so it'll take a little longer." she said. Carl groaned and lifted his right hand. It was twisted one hundred eighty degrees in the wrong direction.

"Looks like I won't be fighting any time soon," he whimpered. "How long will it take?"

"At least three days, but I can treat it every day. Plus some traditional healing and it'll be fine by tomorrow." Cleo assured.

"Ready to go!" Rowan shouted from the Cove Guardian's corpse. He held up the bottle, which was half filled with a glowing periwinkle colored liquid. Cleo and Aiden helped Carl to his feet. Arella walked ahead.

. . .

"What now?" Cleo asked once they were aboard their mounts. Rowan glanced at the bottle in his hands and put on a determined expression.

"Next we locate the map that'll lead us to the portal frame. But let's think. Where do we think it is?" No one said a word. Once she thought about it, it was actually very difficult to think of where she thought something was because she was always used to finding things by looking in the least expected places.

"Wait. Is it, like, magical or something?" Carl asked. Arella nodded.

"It's enchanted to find whoever's after it. All we need to do is find it where we think it is."

Again nobody said a thing. And then Ezra began rummaging through the saddle pack behind his leopard's saddle.

"Nothing in Floopy's pack," he said.

"You named your leopard Floopy?" Cleo scoffed.

"Yeah. Anyways, I thought the map would be in my saddle pack because that's where I would find almost all of my lost items. It's a common place." Then everyone started searching their personal packs. All except for Cleo, of course. She didn't even have a saddle.

.   .   .

After hours of searching the obvious places, Cleo was ready to give up.

"This is getting nowhere," Carl agreed. If the map was exactly where they thought it was, then why wasn't it?

Then it hit her.

"Hey, Ezra. You said you always find your things in your saddle pack because they always get lost there, right? Well I once left my dagger in the fridge. Another time I left it under my bed." She stated.

"What are you saying?" Rowan asked.

"That she's really good at losing her daggers?" Carl offered.

"No," Cleo, Rowan, Arella, Tamsyn, Ezra, and Aiden all said at the same time.

"I'm saying that whenever you need to find something, it's always where you never thought it would be." she explained. "Over time, you learn to look in unobvious places. Earlier I was thinking about why it was so hard to think of where it could be because I was so used to looking exactly where I didn't think something could be. So to find this map, we need to think of where we think it is. And where do we think every lost item is?"

"In the place where you least expect it," Aiden finished.

"Exactly. And what's the last place you would look for the map?" Rowan shrunk down a little.

"Back at the Cove," he said. "The map is right where we started."

CHAPTER 14

Cleo didn't want to return to the cove. After riding a monster, being smashed against a rock wall, almost dying three times, seeing her friend be smashed against a wall, casting an exhausting advanced spell, and killing the monster, the cove was the last place she wanted to see right now. Thankfully, Rowan understood and let her stay with the animals with Tamsyn while the rest went to get the map. She didn't understand why they all had to go together. Couldn't just one or two leave while the rest stayed behind? Seriously.

Tamsyn was sharpening her two daggers with the flintstone that was used to start fires. Sparks crackled from the blades.

"So," Cleo began. "How's life?"

"Good," Tamsyn replied in a shrill voice, not looking up from her work. Cleo nodded and looked down. There was nothing to do, so she decided to make something for Solfang so riding him would be a little more comfortable for him. She asked to borrow Tamsyn's secondary weapon, her axe. She chopped a flexible twig from a nearby bush and whittled it into a curved shape with one of her swords. She tied it down with some strips of smooth leather and strapped them to Solfang's back. Now to steer him, she wouldn't need to reach all the way to his horns, she would just need to pull the stick to one side and her dragon would understand.

It took only about half an hour for her little craft, and again she was left bored again. What was taking the others so long? Then a loud sound rang through the land.

STOMP... STOMP... STOMP ...

Cleo looked up to locate the noise and found herself staring at a familiar face around one hundred feet away. It took her a few seconds to realize who she was looking at.

Elrod.

In only a few seconds they were within earshot and Cleo could hear the master mage cursing and muttering to himself.

"Stupid mage. Stupid plan. Stupid promise." He and his companions reached the hero camp in a few seconds. He spotted Cleo and Tamsyn staring at them and put on a sly expression.

"Excuse me, young ladies," he started. "But do you happen to have seen a young girl with long black hair and murderous eyes?" Tamsyn shook her head, but Cleo gulped, frozen and unable to move. Elrod was looking for her. He had actually left the fortress to find her.

"No, sir," Tamsyn said, but she looked as though she remembered something. Elrod grinned, and Cleo knew what was coming. If he had the slightest suspicion about anyone or anything, he would lash out. She had to protect her friend.

But she was too late.

Elrod held out his hand and clenched his fingers into a fist as though he were squeezing an egg. Immediately Tamsyn started levitating, choking and gagging while clutching her throat like she was being hanged. In a few minutes she would choke to death.

"Wait," Cleo interjected as calmly as she could, but she felt her voice shaking. Elrod opened his hand and Tamsyn dropped to the ground, coughing and wheezing.

"Explain," he sneered coldly. "I know you're hiding something." Cleo took a worried glance at Tamsyn who struggled to her feet, still clutching her throat. She had a plan, but she needed to trust Tamsyn with her life for it.

She took off her disguise and heard Tamsyn gasp in her quiet voice.

"Carl. . ," she trailed off. Eradoa nodded without turning her head. Even Elrod, the wisest of the five leaders, had wide eyes. Then all of a sudden he put on an angry face.

"Eradoa you directly disobeyed every rule set in my fortress. If you were not my favorite student I would have..."

"No need to finish that." Eradoa said. "You have to trust me."

Eradoa wasn't scared. She was terrified.

Elrod was a master mage, the highest of all the high mages in the fortress. He could break her arm with the snap of his fingers, wring her neck in less than two seconds. She was lucky to still be alive.

"I heard the captive muttering in his sleep." She didn't say what; she didn't want to give Elrod any information.

"The captive...Carl?" Tamsyn muttered quietly.

"I let him escape so I could follow him." Eradoa continued. "He led me here."

She explained the rest of the story as quickly and briefly as she could, without giving away any info about the map or the potion. She decided to also keep the elephant part to herself, in case Elrod and the others decided to capture it and keep it for themselves.

"Elrod, this was all just a con mission. To get to know the heroes from the inside. But now this one knows about it all." she said, pointing at Tamsyn, who was wide eyed. "And it's *your* fault." Elrod didn't soften his gaze, which felt like needles punching into ice.

"I was *going* to come back and send someone else for the job, but it was going great and I'd already gained their trust. And now *you* come along and threaten to ruin it all."

Elrod narrowed his eyes.

"What are you implying?" he asked.

"I'm implying," Eradoa said, "that you let me continue the mission. I'll figure out what to do with her." She jerked her head at Tamsyn, who was visibly trembling, but tried not to show her fear.

"Very well," Elrod said. "But I would have appreciated it if you had let me know of this mission of yours a little sooner. I'm afraid we'll have to...discard that one." He looked down at Tamsyn. She had her daggers raised, but being surrounded by enemies with crazy powers was enough to make even Rowan's bones tremble.

"Hey," Eradoa interrupted. "We can use her. If you teach me that memory wiping spell I used to pester you about, I can remove this conversation from her mind and get whatever information we need." Elrod thought for a moment.

"Hmm. Killing her would be the more sensible choice." he mumbled. Eradoa shook her head.

"The others think I'm alone with her right now. If they come back to see her dead or missing they'll start to suspect me." Elrod thought for a while.

"Fine. She'll live for now, and I'll give you the spell. Do not let anything slip. I will not be this lenient the next time we cross paths." He handed her a scroll the color of burnt bread that read: TOROLEM HEPHTERUS. Then he turned to leave.

"Elrod, wait. You need to know something. Whatever you do, don't think about using any sort of spell to try and locate me. I'll be on the constant move and trying to find me will make the heroes suspicious. They're smarter than you think. Just keep minding your own business and don't think of me." she said.

"But what will I tell the other leaders?" Elrod asked.

"Just tell them that I'm undercover and you didn't want to interfere. Kaska will most likely buy that and she'll convince the others, too." she suggested. "Neroon might argue, though." Elrod nodded and turned around.

"I can handle Neroon. Do not fail." He said, then muttered to himself, "too much is at stake."

Then he turned himself and his companions into eagles and flew off.

Eradoa looked back at Tamsyn who was as terrified as a bunny surrounded by a pack of foxes. But as soon as the eagles were no longer visible she let out a relieved sigh.

"Finally they're gone," she said, walked over to Eradoa, and punched her square in the jaw. Eradoa fell over, then stood up again.

"Ow," she moaned.

"I feel better now. Nice job double crossing them, by the way." Tamsyn squeaked in her high voice.

"How do you know I was double crossing them?" Eradoa asked.

"I can tell. I've done that before." She said.

"So you were pretending to be scared?"

"Yup. If that freaky dude thought I was helpless and weak, it would give me an advantage if I had to fight."

"Oh, you can't fight Elrod." Eradoa said. "Trust me."

"I'm stronger than I look." Tamsyn said, frowning. "And I doubt he could land one hit on me." Eradoa agreed—she'd seen Tamsyn in action during the battle with the Cove Guardian. But Elrod could do crazy things, and all the heroes plus Eradoa wouldn't stand a chance against him.

Eradoa got ready to put her disguise back on when Aiden came running. He stopped and caught his breath.

"Cleo, Tamsyn. Help. Something major's happ. . ,"
he stopped when he noticed Eradoa in her robes and
with black hair. His eyes widened. "Wait. You're the
mage Carl was talking about! Where's Cleo?!" he
shouted. Eradoa sighed and rolled her eyes. She waved
her hand in front of her face and she shrunk into
Cleo's form.

"I *am* Cleo, you idiot," she said. Aiden came
forward and punched her in the face.

"Much better," he said. "Cool that you're double
crossing them, but I really needed to do that." Cleo
stood up and nodded.

"Good to know. Anyways, what happened?
What's the rush?" she asked. Aiden said nothing and
took off. Tamsyn and Cleo followed him into the Cove.

. . .

Aiden led them to the back of the Cove. In front of them was a wall of boulders that looked like they had fallen from the ceiling. Aiden began to explain what had happened.

"We found another cavern. They wanted to explore so I volunteered to stay behind and notify you guys later on, just in case something happened. Turns out the place was unstable and these huge rocks came thundering down." He explained.

"But where's everyone else?" Cleo asked.

"That's the thing." Aiden said. "They're trapped inside."

CHAPTER 15

"You mean the others are all behind layers of boulders and are stuck there until we stumble upon someone or something strong enough to break thousands of tons' worth of rock?" Cleo asked incredulously. She groaned when Aiden nodded.

"Can't you, like, float the rocks away or something?" he asked.

"Nope. I can do a few magic tricks but I'm not telekinetic. Well I am, sort of, but I can't do *that*." she replied. Then she had an idea. She dashed outside, leaving the others clueless. She whistled, calling Solfang to her. She held her hand up and felt her dragon pick her up and fling her onto his back. She flew him to the top of the Cove and noticed a portion of it extruding from the back.

Once she thought about it, the Cove wasn't really a cove, it was more of a ginormous cavern. It was just called the Cove for some reason.

Solfang spit fire. A clump of rock spilled off from the heat. Perfect. If this part of the cavern was as unstable as Aiden had said, it would be easier to break through here than the rest.

But fire alone wouldn't be enough to break through. She needed force from the inside. She dropped to the Cove ceiling and made her way to the little hole Solfang's fire had created.

"HEY!" she yelled, crouching down. "CAN YOU HEAR ME?" She waited a while until a faint answer returned.

"Yeah! We're here!" Rowan's voice responded.

"THROW YOUR WEAPONS UP! QUICKLY!" she yelled back. She got to her feet and climbed back onto her dragon, who continued to shoot fire from his mouth. The rock began to crack and crumble and Cleo could hear the swords and daggers and axes clanging from inside. She wondered how long it would take for them to find their own weapons after the rocks broke down and sprayed dust everywhere.

After around twenty minutes of blasting, Solfang was out of firepower. He couldn't blast any more, and he was bone-tired from flying and blasting at the same time. He plopped down on the roof of the Cove, exhausted.

But the moment he got down the entire roof of the cave collapsed and layers of rock and stone fell down the sides of the cavern, leaving a huge thirty-foot hole in the center. Below were four coughing teens with no weapons.

"Hurry up and get out of there!" Cleo yelled. She hopped off her dead-tired dragon and onto the dry grassy ground.

The others dug up their weapons—with a little help from Cleo's weak telekinetic powers—and climbed out.

Soon everyone was out and okay, though Carl said something had hit his broken wrist. Cleo put a simple soothing spell on it to help it heal a little faster.

"What now?" Arella asked.

"Now we follow the map," Rowan replied, holding a red scroll case in his hand.

"I wonder how that monster held so many valuable items in its stomach for millennia without vomiting." Carl muttered.

Rowan insisted that they would travel on foot as Solfang was tired and wouldn't be able to fly for a while, since Selkath wouldn't be able to carry all of them. They all climbed aboard their animals. Rowan offered to let Cleo ride with him, since Solfang was drained of all his energy, and could barely slink alongside them. Rowan took out a sack of food rations from his saddle pack and tossed the dragon a chunk of meat. He caught it up and swallowed it happily, hanging his mouth open for more. Rowan handed the sack to Cleo.

"Where's the red X?" she asked, looking at the map and tossing Solfang some meat. "X marks the spot,"

"There isn't any. Where in the world did you hear about a red X??" Rowan asked. "The blue square marks the spot." He showed her the map. Sure enough, there was a blue rectangle surrounding an oasis in a desert not far from where they were.

"Hey guys," Arella said. "Solfang looks like he's about to die." Cleo looked back at him, or at least where he used to be. He had lagged behind at least ten meters, and was barely able to walk. Cleo gasped, worried.

Then Arella did something unexpected. She pulled a necklace from under her combat armor and whispered something silently. Selkath began to glow and vaporized into a dark blue twirl of light that zapped into the opal pendant of the necklace. Cleo was impressed.

"Woah, since when can you do that?"

"Since forever. It's my way of protecting Selkath and keeping him close." Arella replied. She pointed at Solfang and did the same for him, vaporizing him into her pendant. "Now he can rest."

Rowan waved for everyone to move faster. Soon, everyone had broken into a run.

.   .   .

"The Midnight Desert," Rowan said. "Said to be nighttime here all the time." Sure enough, the sky was black with thousands of stars.

"Great. We get in, find the portal, light it, save the Archmage Arcanum, and kill a bunch of bad guys that'll probably try to kill us. No problem. Give me a week." Carl uttered sarcastically, but everyone's face stayed the same.

"Hey, what's so bad about this desert? Just a bunch of sand, right?" Cleo asked.

"Well, yes," Arella said, almost whispering. "Except for the Spirit Fangs."

"Wait, you mean someone's gonna copy my dragon a gazillion times and all I have to do is say, 'heel!'?" she joked. Arella tucked her necklace back into her armor.

"No, *Spirit* Fangs. Spirit, not Soul. Deadly winged snakes."

"How do we kill them?"

"We can't. They have a lifespan of about two hours, but they lay hundreds of eggs within the first half."

"Plus one bite will drive you mad within minutes," Carl added. Cleo slid off Rowan's lion— Ayala's—back. Immediately something under the sand slithered and sprang up. It was half black, half navy blue with silver spines, like a dragon's, and two large bat wings sprouting from its back.

Right before its deadly fangs sank into her shin, Cleo pulled out a sword and sliced it in half. It dropped to the ground and disintegrated into a pile of black dust that was blown away by the desert wind.

"Careful," Rowan said. "The animals can sense exactly where they are, so it's best to stay on for now." Cleo nodded and pulled herself back on.

Wind blew her hair in her face and tickled her skin. Despite that, she still felt unnaturally warm, like her insides were being roasted over a fire.

Suddenly Rowan stopped, taking the bottle of magic liquid out of his saddle pack. It was glowing white hot.

"What's wrong?" Tamsyn asked from her horse. In the moonlight, it looked especially majestic.

"The bottle's feeling really warm," Rowan replied. Then he dropped the bottle back into his pack and shook his hand like he'd been burned. "Sorry, I've been feeling like the thing's on fire ever since we entered the Midnight Desert."

They walked on, following the map to the blue rectangle at the furthest corner of the desert. Cleo asked why they couldn't just fly over the desert as it would be faster, plus Solfang would be rested by now with all his fire to blast the snakes to smithereens. But he simply pointed to the sky and said,

"Spirit fangs are blind, but they have an extraordinary sense of smell." Sure enough, there were several of the snakes flapping around in the sky. Cleo wondered what would happen if one decided to land.

They walked for hours and nothing moved but the writhing snakes beneath their feet. The gibbous moon stayed high in the night sky, or maybe high in the day sky. Honestly, it was hard to tell. Every once in a while Cleo looked to one of the others to see how well they were coping with this kind of boredom. Arella seemed to be slouching and Aiden and Ezra were half asleep. That being said, it was most likely nighttime.

"Stop," Rowan said suddenly. "This is it,"

"What?"

"The portal. It's here."

CHAPTER 16

"Where? I don't see anything." Aiden said. Rowan stared at the map.

"I don't understand. It should be right here. Unless it's below us, of course." He scooped up a handful of sand. Underneath was a thin layer of purplish-orange sand.

"Wait, if the portal is below us then why is this weird dust up here?" Cleo asked. Rowan shrugged.

"It's a magic portal. Of course it does weird things that none of us can explain, because portals. . .um. . .do that all the time, I guess? " Arella tapped her necklace twice and both Solfang and Selkath were zapped out.

"Let's start digging," she said. Then all of a sudden a snake lunged from the ground with its fangs bared. Arella brought her hand up and froze the snake in midair.

"Careful," Cleo warned. "Don't get used to using magic. It's more unpredictable than you think." The thought reminded her of the time around five months ago when she fought a chimera, a beast with a lion's head, goat's body, and a snake for a tail. She used a flame spell to counter its attack when she turned her thumb only a half centimeter too far. The spell exploded in a burst of fire that roasted her skin and threw her back against a tree. Not only was she burned badly, but her impact with the tree left her with a broken arm and a fractured toe. She was in sick bay for almost two weeks. She was lucky magic existed and doctors were trained in healing spells and botany, otherwise she would still be there now. But those two weeks of being in sick bay, she was scared that the healers would accidentally blast her nose off with their spells.

Arella set her bird to claw a little deeper into the ground. More of the dusty purple sand was revealed (and a few snakes), but no portal. Half an hour later, after digging up over ten feet of sand, all they found were more Spirit fangs.

"I don't get it." Arella said. "Is the map wrong?"

"No, it can't be. We'll just have to keep digging." Rowan replied, but Cleo didn't think this was going to get anywhere.

In around an hour, there was a huge hole in the ground. The only change was that the purple dust came in layers maybe a few millimeters each and then a layer of normal sand about five inches, then another dust layer, then sand, and the pattern repeated like the stripes of a tiger. But the portal was nowhere to be seen. She told Rowan she didn't believe the portal to be under them, but he shook his head and continued digging.

"Where else could it be?"

Another fifteen minutes passed and still, no one found anything. Even worse, there were so many Spirit fangs here, it looked like a snake breeding point. It was nothing too bad, except that one almost drove its teeth into Solfang's forearm. But as it turned out, they were not fireproof. So Solfang was set to Spirit Fang incinerating duty, while the rest of them, including Selkath, continued to dig.

But that wasn't the only close incident with the snakes. One of them slithered into Floopy's saddle pack and started knocking things out. Piles of gold coins, old parchments, and road snacks lay on the floor. There was also a very peculiar selfie of Ezra and a monkey doing silly faces. Ezra blushed and took the snake out. He slit its throat and started putting everything back, thinking everything was normal. But it wasn't.

Cleo stared into the leopard's eyes. They had changed from icy blue to stormy gray. Floopy leaped up and sank his teeth into Ezra's shoulder. Instantly his eyes turned gray as well and he drew his sword.

It took a moment for Cleo to realize what had happened. Floopy had been bitten by the snake, been driven mad enough to attack Ezra, and now Ezra was crazy too. He sliced his arm and let the blood flow onto his blade. Whoever did so much as touch the blade now would face the same fate. Even worse, as far as any one of them knew, there was no antidote to Spirit fang venom.

Except for the one thing that could cure anything.

Cleo took out the old shard of tusk from the Elephant of Doom, the one she'd sheared off and didn't even need. She brought out her sword and got as close to Ezra as she could without touching his blood-covered weapon. He struck at her again and again, and it was hard to believe someone into botany and medicine could fight this well. Unfortunately for him, Cleo had the advantage—him being crazy and vulnerable and all—, and with only three strong blows of her blade, knocked the sword out of his hands.

His expression shifted from wild to wilder as he took out two daggers and slashed at her face. She dodged each of his attacks and sheathed her sword. She wouldn't be able to deflect the small knives with her long blade, plus she didn't want to hurt Ezra by accident.

Ezra brought a dagger down on her head but she grabbed his wrist, turned him around and kicked the back on his knee. He fell face-flat on the sand, but got up quickly. Again he attacked, this time with both daggers. Cleo took hold of one dagger right above where Ezra was holding it, and bashed his chin with her knee before the other one hit her. Ezra stumbled back and attacked again. This time, Cleo jumped to one side, and slid two fingers to his temples. She whispered a spell and his whole face flashed blue. He buckled over and his body went stiff.

"Okay, that should take care of that for now," she said out loud.

"Did you kill him?" Carl asked.

"No, of course not. He's just paralyzed for about five minutes. But be on guard, he'll be up soon. And were you guys just watching over there?"

"Um. . .you seemed to have it under control?" Tamsyn said.

"Ugh. Anyways, there's a psychopathic clouded leopard standing right behind you with its teeth bared, and I think you should do something." They turned and looked. Sure enough, Floopy was there, ready for the kill. He lunged at Aiden, but missed as he ducked under and rolled to one side. And as the leopard ran at Tamsyn, she did a backflip over its flank and kicked it back. While they all took turns dodging and tiring Floopy, Cleo sat back and watched it like a movie, dodging and slicing in half the occasional attacking Spirit fang.

In a few minutes things settled and Floopy was being held down. Cleo walked over with the shard of tusk and hit it with the hilt of her sword. Dust fell onto where the leopard had been bitten and his eyes turned back to normal. But that was the bad thing.

Cleo had let her guard down and had totally forgotten about Ezra who was unconscious behind her. Right when she slipped her sword into its sheath he sprang up and tackled her. She was taken by surprise and didn't have time to react, but when she finally realized that Ezra was awake, she easily threw him off. He rolled to his feet and lunged at Rowan who had his back turned. What didn't make sense was that Ezra didn't draw his sword. He merely knocked Rowan over and grabbed the map right out of his hands.

"Thanks," he said, then ran off into nowhere.

CHAPTER 17

Rowan instantly got to his feet and ran after Ezra while Cleo climbed onto Solfang's back. Both raced after him, wondering what he wanted with the map. Twenty feet into the air, she remembered the tusk shard. She had left it behind, but at the speed in which Ezra was running at, she didn't have time to go get it.

She gained on him fast and was about to grab him when she noticed something horrifying in front of her.

A large pit teeming with Spirit fangs lay in front of her. Ezra dove in and was caught by maybe ten snakes that carried him to the center of the pit, where he recited something that sounded like a summoning hex. Cleo remembered the invisibility potion on her belt and took a sip. Her body faded away and she climbed down the steep side of the pit.

The terrifying part was that there was a sixty foot drop into a den of Spirit fangs from where she was and that would probably, most definitely, kill her.

And that would be a bad thing.

She made her way down the last few feet of the den wall and carefully stepped over the snakes slithering around her feet until Ezra stood only four yards ahead. He stopped chanting and a gentle breeze started to blow. Soon the breeze grew into a strong wind and the wind turned into a storm.

It was strong enough to blow Cleo off her feet. She was pushed toward the south and the only thing keeping her from getting blown into the snakes behind her was the small stone sticking out from the ground that she was holding onto.

The only one who remained standing was Ezra, yet he was crouching down with his back towards the source of the wind, which was only a few feet ahead of where he was. Also in front of Ezra, there was a groove in the shape of two ellipses crossed together. It began to glow bright blue and a beam of light extended in a cylindrical shape.

Finally, Ezra was overwhelmed and was thrown back by the wind, which felt like the sting of a million hornets.

Suddenly with a loud shrill, the column of light disappeared, and a dome of blue light flashed. Cleo assumed that nothing could be seen or heard outside of the dome. Along with the beam, the wind came to a sudden halt as well.

Ezra stood up. Nothing seemed to happen for a few unbearably quiet moments, until another scream rang through the den. In the center of the crossed ellipses stood a giant Spirit fang coiled up as though it were asleep. It was *huge*.

It was a deep purplish-gray color with a black tongue that flicked in and out of its mouth. Its hood was at least fifty yards wide and made the snake look so much bigger. It had no spikes, unlike the other tiny Spirit fangs, but had two enormous wings that probably could have blown away all the sand in the Midnight Desert with one flap.

The snake raised its head and opened its eyes, which were dark red. Then it spoke in a female voice mixed with hisses that sent chills down Cleo's spine.

Which blueberry muffin dares summon me to my least favorite napping spot? It said. Ezra stepped up and kneeled, his head bowed.

"I, your majesty,"

And for what?

"I have an interesting artifact you may want to see." He held up the map. "As you can see, another group of 'brave heroes' is trying to rescue the mage Arcanum, as you might have guessed. But they aren't as bad as they look."

Hmm?

"Yes, your majesty. They have a dragon and Blue Phoenix on their side, plus near-impenetrable armor. Believe me, I'm wearing it."

Is that so? Well that 'impenetrable armor' must have a weakness, yes?

"Yes. It is vulnerable to magic." The giant snake flickered its tongue.

Then in that case it should be easy wiping them out, just like everyone else. The thought made Cleo shiver, not wanting to know what the snake meant when she said, 'everyone else'.

"Yes, but there's another problem. They have a mage, too. One that may just be a match for you." Cleo was flattered, but decided to never put a fight with a huge Spirit fang on her to-do list.

You, muffin, have still not explained why you have summoned me. This is by far the most uncomfortable place to nap, and until you leave my den, I may not return to my fluffy bed of monkey skins. Ezra gulped.

"Well, your majesty. These heroes stand a fighting chance for reaching their destination. It's only a matter of time before they find the portal. You'll need to stop them."

And why, in the name of cinnamon swirl cupcakes, would I need to get my scales dirty for something that has never happened, and never will happen? No matter how skilled anyone calls themselves, they will never be clever enough for what lies beyond that portal. Assuming you know what that is. Ezra moistened his lips.

"No, your majesty." The giant snake brought her head back and opened her mouth. Cleo was itching to know what this 'life-threatening obstacle' was. And of course, her hopes were crushed.

Bah. Why did I think you would know? You're one of them. Whatever. If these heroes are really so 'skilled', then might as well get rid of them. Come. The snake slithered forward and Ezra trailed along. Only after she was completely uncoiled did Cleo see how big she really was. From her head to the tip of her tail, she was maybe two hundred times Solfang's size.

Then all of a sudden, the snake lifted her head sharply, as if someone had stabbed a needle into her neck. She tasted the air and hissed.

There's someone here. Then she muttered something in a language of hisses and a wave of cyan light spread across the dome. Cleo's invisibility spell ripped off like shedding dragon scales. Ezra's face contorted.

"What the—," he said. Cleo grinned sheepishly.

The Spirit fangs around her started to hiss.

Well well, looks like we have a guest. The giant snake hissed, and slithered forward until she was only a few feet from Cleo's face. She lowered her head and flicked her tongue.

"Queen Hemera, this is all the more reason to go after the heroes. This one's heard everything." Ezra suggested. Something about that made a click at her brain. Queen Hemera, he said?

She focused on the snake in front of her, who had moved so close that her tongue looked doubled. Realization hit her with the force of a thousand suns. Cleo was face to face with the queen of the Spirit fangs.

CHAPTER 18

Cleo didn't recall exactly what had happened, but one moment she was about to be eaten alive and in the next she was being plucked from the ground and sent flying.

Probably some freak magic that came from the snake queen. How would she defeat something that could knock her back twenty miles with a single hit? Was that even possible? But that was a problem for a Cleo who was not currently ninety feet in the air. She had maybe one or two minutes before she went *ker-splat* on the desert sands.

The only good part was that coincidentally, she was headed straight for Rowan and the others, but it would be a bad thing if she fell on them.

She remembered at nearly the last moment that she had a levitation potion in her tool belt. She fumbled for it and yanked off the cork. Right before she smashed into Solfang's face, a drop fell into her mouth and she floated over his head. Everyone turned to look at her.

"'Sup?" she grinned sheepishly. Carl walked up holding the tusk shard.

"You forgot this," he said.

"I know, but we've got bigger problems." Cleo said as she floated to the ground. She tried to place her feet down, but they repelled from the ground like magnets. "And now I can't stand normally. Solfang, you get a break." The dragon let out a puff of smoke. Cleo didn't know exactly what he was saying, but she could guess it was some sarcastic remark, and she punched his forearm. That sent her flying back several feet.

"Where's Ezra?" Carl asked. Cleo took the shard and stared at her reflection in the shiny surface. She only saw a failure before her.

"Turns out, getting bitten by a Spirit fang doesn't drive you mad. It turns you into another Spirit fang.

You become loyal to the snake leader, Queen Hemera." She said.

"They have a *queen?*" Tansym yelped. Cleo nodded.

"You don't want to meet her."

"Tell me you at least got some information,"

"You bet. But now she and Ezra are coming for us. And if I'm a mage, I know what she'll do next."

A few moments later, the Spirit fang queen appeared before them through a teleportation spell, just as Cleo had predicted. She was even bigger than Cleo remembered, and looked more than twice as sinister, though that first part may have just been her imagination. Her black tongue flicked in and out, spewing poison on the ground that missed Selkath's tail by an inch. He squawked and flew over to Arella's side.

We meet again, Eradoa. The queen said.

Cleo held her breath.

"What the—," she took a quick glance at Carl behind her, who looked equally as surprised, but more scared.

"Cleo?" he muttered quietly. She drew her swords.

Oh, those aren't going to do anything to me, little muffin.

"How do you know my name?"

I know many things. Didn't Elrod tell you how important you are?

"Cleo?" Rowan said in a low, careful voice. "What is she talking about?"

"She really doesn't know." Arella said, saving her from answering.

"I'll tell all of you later." Cleo promised.

Ezra popped out from behind the snake. He looked shaken up, most likely because he had never been through a teleportation spell. Cleo knew why. It was one of the more complicated spells that even she couldn't do. The first time she experienced it was when master mage Elrod used it on her to bring her to the fortress on her fourteenth birthday. It had pretty much knocked her out.

Ezra's skin had turned purple and fangs the size of his fingers were sticking out from the edges of his mouth. The transformation was beginning.

Cleo sneaked closer to Rowan.

"What do we do?" she whispered.

"I thought you had the info!" he replied. "*You're* the evil one, not me." Cleo could sense the fear in his tone.

"I'm not evil. And all I know is that she has a thick hide that repels spells, and her scales can deflect any melee weapon. Our attacks are all useless."

"Very helpful,"

Hemera lunged, baring her fangs. The attack wasn't aimed at Cleo, but she was thrown back as if the queen had cast some sort of spell. The sand gave her a soft landing, but the others weren't so lucky. Tamsyn and Carl were up several feet in the air, so far that their screams were only as loud as buzzing flies.

Solfang caught them and brought them to the ground, and Selkath went after Rowan, Arella, and Aiden. He caught Rowan and Arella, but didn't get to Aiden in time. He fell, screaming, towards the ground, while Hemera slithered after him, ready to kill. Cleo was helping the others to the ground, and was too late to see Aiden falling to his death. She turned to Arella, who already had her eyes closed. She held out her hand as if she were choking someone and clenched her hand into a fist.

Cleo looked toward Aiden. He crashed to the ground, but instead of hitting the sand, he floated just millimeters above it. Arella opened her eyes and brought her hand in. Aiden came flying toward them and slammed into Solfang's side, who toppled over and spilled everyone onto the ground.

"Whoa. Arella, tha—," Cleo began, and then realized that Hemera was coming at them a hundred miles an hour. "And we're in trouble." Arella closed her eyes again and waved her hand over her head. A force field appeared over them. When Hemera came, her jaws clamped over the protection dome.

"This won't hold forever," Cleo said. "The more force Hemera puts on this dome, the more tired Arella will get. We need to get her out of here before she passes out." Cleo put her hand out and did a 360, landing on one knee with her hand planted on the ground. Just as the bubble popped, everything inside the force field disappeared and reappeared behind the queen. Aiden pulled out his sword and stabbed it into Hemera's tail. It harmlessly bounced off, but it caught the snake's attention.

There you are. Now, I'm under the impression that cupcakes are meant to be eaten!

She lunged again and they all dove out of the way. Arella looked like a zombie.

"Selkath, get her out of here!" Rowan screamed. The bird squawked and grabbed Arella by the leg. As he flew away, Arella dropped a crossbow loaded with one arrow.

"Cleo, what are you thinking!? We need everyone here!" Rowan yelled.

"She's gonna die, you bonehead!" Cleo yelled back.

Before they had any more time to argue, Hemera slithered up and expanded her hood, making herself look twice as large and four times as evil.

Say goodbye! She sneered, and opened her mouth to spray her poison. Cleo had two seconds to think, just enough time for her guts to come up with something stupid. She grabbed Arella's crossbow and fired the single arrow into Hemera's right eye. The snake queen screamed a blood-curdling scream of hisses and snarls.

Cleo and Rowan pulled everyone else away. The arrow had bought them enough time to make an escape.

Soon the arrow fell out and Hemera got her head back into the game. She hissed and spun around, whacking her tail into anything in its path. Luckily, she only had one eye and didn't realize that there was no one there. Cleo hopped onto Solfang's back and slipped off almost immediately, remembering that her levitation potion had lingering effects.

Aiden was running by with his sword out and Cleo gestured to him. Solfang nodded and grabbed him by the leather scabbard on his back. He flung him at Hemera's face. Aiden, with his arm still out, flew at the queen's head. His blade took out her other eye and she screamed again. Aiden was thrown off her head, but he landed with a soft thud on the sand.

Hemera stood there, wailing and hissing curses that would have earned her an award at the fortress.

But even after all that, she still looked as powerful as ever.

Cleo watched Rowan and Aiden charged at Ezra, who had been trying to infect them. Both of them together were able to pin him down, but he had the added strength of a Spirit fang. He thrashed and flailed, almost throwing them both off.

Cleo found the tusk shard and brought it over to them. She banged the hilt of her sword against the edge and a few flakes drifted down into Ezra's mouth.

Almost instantly his fangs disappeared and his skin turned back to normal.

"Dude, you look a lot better now that you're not turning into a snake." Carl commented.

"All in favor of shoving Carl into a volcano?" Rowan intervened, and everyone raised their hand.

"But it's true, actually. I feel better, too." Ezra said.

Cleo laughed.

"Anyways, we have a giant queen to take down, so let's get to work. Ezra, do you know anything about snakes?"

"Yes I do. Their weakness is the cold because they're cold blooded."

"Wait. Was that a fact or an insult?" Aiden joked.

"Ha ha, very funny. Let's go."

Cleo conjured up a basic ice spell and blasted it at Hemera's underbelly. It hardly did a thing. She needed a more powerful spell, or she needed to weaken the queen first. Neither of those were going to be easy, but searching for a powerful spell would give her a more likely chance of not fulfilling the purpose of a cupcake.

Then she remembered that she had stuffed a spellbook in one of her neverending pockets in her tool belt. She pulled it out and flipped to a chapter on ice spells. They all were either too complicated to do at her level or weren't strong enough to take down Hemera.

Then an idea hit her.

She had never liked the rain because it was wet and hard to fight in. But most of all she hated the cold. Weather spells were particularly easy, so a simple thunderstorm wouldn't take too much energy. She recited the spell,

"Notus silavare," and the sky began to rumble. A huge storm was coming, one big enough to hopefully take down the queen, or at least distract her enough for them to escape without her noticing. Thunder clouds rolled into the sky, and lightning flashed.

But something was wrong.

Instead of normal rain, the clouds released shards of ice. And instead of crashing down and shattering, they exploded in midair, right above everyone's heads.

The clouds turned into red fire. The ice got bigger. The air turned toxic.

Uh oh.

She'd done the spell wrong. Instead of emphasizing the *notus*, she emphasized the *silavare*. When using magic, she had to be very careful with pronunciation, or it could worsen the effect. Yes, this was a problem.

In a few seconds, the air would be too toxic to breathe, they would get exploded by ice, or they would get incinerated, plus the always-welcome option of being the queen's dessert. In a few seconds, if she didn't find a way to stop this, they would all be in heaven.

CHAPTER 19

Notus Silavare. Notus Silavare. Notus Silavare.
Cleo muttered over and over. Nothing changed.

Guys, take cover!" Cleo yelled. The storm had started to pick up. The wind was like needles and the ice rain would be even worse. The only one who was in a worse condition than Cleo and the others was Hemera, who was writhing with her hood down.

She hissed and snarled every time a shard of ice exploded on her. At least one part of the plan had worked.

Cleo found this as a perfect opportunity to take off, leaving the queen alone in the storm, but she couldn't get to everyone, and Solfang wouldn't be able to fly in this wind.

The wind got stronger and Cleo was blown off her feet. She grabbed one of her swords and stuck it as deep as she could into the sand, hanging on like her life depended on it.

Just when she thought the circumstances couldn't get any worse, they did. In the distance, the winds began to swirl around. So many currents going in the same direction had formed a tornado.

And it was headed right for them.

"Help!" said a small voice from below her. It was Aiden, clinging onto a small rock in the ground. Cleo pulled herself up until her waist was at her sword and hung on with her legs. Now that she had turned around, she could see that Aiden's rock was about to pop out of the ground. She grabbed Aiden's wrist just as it fell out and pulled him onto her sword. They caught their breaths for a few moments, and then Cleo's heart stopped again when she felt her sword losing its grip from the ground. She brought out her other one and stuck it, grabbing onto both.

The tornado was getting closer. Aiden yelled something, but was drowned out by the roars of the storm. In only a few seconds they would be sucked into the vortex.

Five. . .

Four. . .

Three. . .

Two. . .

One. . .

Cleo and Aiden were still holding onto the swords when the tornado caught them. Cleo felt like her insides were being churned through a blender. There were some incidents where tornados picked up eggs and dropped them without a single one broken, but this was definitely not one of them.

Aiden vomited, which did not make things any better.

The tornado picked up an oak tree and whacked it into Cleo's face. She went flying backwards and grabbed a hold of one of its branches. Things came and crashed into the tree, breaking off bits of its branches.

Cleo looked around and found Aiden. He was being tossed around and had his shield in front of him that protected him from incoming objects.

Again, Cleo thought things couldn't get any worse.

And of course, they did.

As the tornado closed in, it sucked up Hemera the snake queen. She was strong enough to peel herself away, but she left blobs of poison in the whirlwind. They caught onto Cleo's oak tree. It withered away, almost taking her hand with it.

Cleo watched Aiden get thrown from the tornado. He landed on the ground hard, and she could tell that he had broken a bone by the way he was writhing on the ground, clutching his knee.

Globs of poison came her way and she dodged to the best of her ability. She had to get out of here soon.

Through the dark winds, she saw Solfang carrying Aiden to the others, who were hanging onto things. Rowan, who had been the closest to the queen, was even holding onto Hemera's scales.

Cleo saw a log coming her way and sliced it in half. The two parts separated and went in two opposite directions around her. And then from behind a huge stone hit her in the head. Her brain surged with pain and her eyes began to black out. She fought the urge to pass out and tried to stay strong. Another piece of shrapnel hit her and opened up a nasty gash across her forehead. Blood dripped into her eyes.

And then a huge red figure loomed over her, snatching her up. She realized soon that it was her dragon, Solfang. He fought the strong winds and pushed out of the storm. And right after they escaped, she blacked out.

CHAPTER 20

When Cleo came back to her senses, she was in the eye of a hurricane. Hemera was nowhere to be seen.

Solfang's red face puffed smoke into her face. She grabbed his wing claw and pulled herself onto her feet. She stood up and scanned her surroundings. The storm was still going, and there were a few familiar faces struck with worry.

"What just happened?" she asked them. She couldn't remember the last five minutes of the fight.

"You got sucked into a tornado." Arella told her.

"Oh, right. I did."

"Ezra," Carl said. "I think that tornado did something bad."

"You bet," Ezra said, smiling. "Do you remember us?"

Cleo nodded.

"We should probably recap some of this," Rowan said. "We don't know how much she remembers."

They told her everything about rescuing Ezra, her casting the thunder spell, Queen Hemera taking her last dying breath before her innards freezing. They each took turns explaining, but she could hear a touch of anger and resentment in all of their voices. And as they explained, she remembered all that had happened. And also why they were angry.

"Carl, I am so sorry. I shouldn't have kept this a secret." she said.

"Well, I got over it." he replied. "Arella explained everything."

"Huh? That fast?"

"Oh, no way. You've been out for three days."

"WHAT?" She sat up and rubbed her forehead.

"Yeah."

Cleo blinked a few times.

"Well then I quit the apologies! We need to leave now!"

She began to walk forward, then slipped again. Walking around was gonna take some getting used to.

Arella whispered to her magic pendant and sucked both Selkath and Solfang in.

"It's best if you don't walk for now. And Solfang's too tired to carry you." she said.

"What else can I do?"

"Well, we've got a deer, horse, leopard, lion, and wolf you can ride. Take your pick." Arella suggested. Cleo looked around. Ezra's leopard didn't seem like it would warm up to her quickly, and deer were shy to new people. After everyone found out about her being Eradoa, she didn't want to be too close to Carl for a while.

"I volunteer," Rowan said, making things a whole lot easier.

"Sure," Cleo replied, and hopped over and mounted the lion. Ayala seemed to remember her from their last ride, and purred happily.

They started to walk to where the map had led them earlier. There was a big ditch where they had tried to find the portal earlier. The layers of purple dust were still there, and there were a few more on top. That didn't make any sense.

Unless. . .

"Hey, I think I know where it is." Cleo said. "Anyone got a bow?" Arella tossed her her crossbow. Ezra gave her some spare arrows. She mounted an arrow into the crossbow and fired up into the sky. When it returned to the ground, it was broken.

"Just as I thought," Cleo muttered. The arrow had hit something in the sky. "The portal isn't buried below. It's up there." she said, painting up.

"So you're saying the portal to Arcanum is in the sky." Carl said. Cleo nodded. Arella released Selkath and flew up.

"She's right! I can feel something up here!" she answered a few moments later. She came back down and released Solfang as well. The others split and climbed aboard. Rowan handed Cleo the liquid from the Cove Guardian. They flew up and Cleo felt around and found one of the edges. She poured the liquid onto the frame of the invisible portal.

Almost immediately, it became visible, glowing in a bright purple-pink color. Particles that looked like fire sparks floated from the frame and swirled up into a collected bundle in the center, then fused to become a bright luminescent bulb of the same color. The bulb burst and lit the portal.

The light died soon, settling to a calm dark red color.

"This is it." Rowan said, the light reflecting in his eyes.

They flew in and braced themselves for the worst.

CHAPTER 21

**After all she'd heard about the "dangers"
behind the portal, Cleo had to admit she was
disappointed** at what she saw.

Cleo and the others made their way through the
portal, expecting monsters and mutants to attack. But
instead of stepping into a battlefield of their
nightmares, they entered into a small round stone
room with circular engravings on the ground. In the
very center of the room stood a pedestal with a beam
of light shining onto a little glass case atop the marble
surface of the pedestal.

Inside the glass case was a withering rose with
no thorns. It cast an eerie blue glow throughout the
entire cave. It was nothing special, but out of nowhere
Cleo felt the urge to walk towards the rose. She slowly
made her way to the center of the room, when she

noticed the others were doing the same. It was as if the rose had cast some sort of spell on them.

Cleo was almost to the innermost ring, when the floor under her dropped. She yelped and instinctively drew a knife from her belt, driving it into the wall. She looked up at the others, who were still staring at the rose. They hadn't even noticed her. So she shouted to the closest people to her.

"Rowan! Carl! Hello? Dying person down here!" But they stayed still, simply watching the rose.

Cleo was trying to think of a way out of here. But then Rowan took a step closer and tumbled over the edge of the once-floor.

Cleo shrieked and caught his arm. He was still in that dazed half-dead state. She gave him a good knee to the stomach. Ah, yes. That woke him up.

"Aah! Oh. It's just you." A few seconds passed before he noticed their predicament. "Oh seal guts! Why does this keep happening to us?"

"Stop making me laugh you idiot, I'm gonna let go." She actually did. But thankfully he caught her foot.

"Thanks a lot," Rowan grumbled, and she giggled.

Cleo racked her brain for a way out of this situation. I mean, hanging hundreds of feet off a wall, holding on for dear life, not the situation most people would want to get into, much less know how to get out of without a rope.

"Can't you, like, conjure a rope or something?" Rowan asked.

"I can try, but I'd need both my hands for it to work properly." Cleo replied. She thought of a rope and made a circular motion with her hands. Her other hand was supposed to grab the rope when it appeared, but that wasn't possible as of now.

The rope appeared in the air above Cleo's sword hand. She caught it with her other hand when it dropped. Then she realized it wasn't a rope at all. It was a flimsy kite string.

Suddenly, an idea hit her.

"Rowan, take my other sword," Cleo said, dropping the string and slipping her crossed sword sheath down low enough for Rowan to grab her second sword. That was the good news. The bad news was that he'd pulled off her shoe and was falling to his death. He stabbed the sword into the wall and held on with both his hands, shivering.

"I was expecting that to happen. So much for my plan." Cleo mumbled.

"Great. Thanks for the early warning."

Cleo giggled again. "Sorry, but right now we have to figure out how to get out of this hole. I can't think of anything. Why are you looking at me like that." Indeed, Rowan was giving her a significant look.

"Well, you're kind of the daring ideas kind of person, so I was hoping you would have a plan."

Cleo thought for a while. Then another idea hit her.

"Okay I do, but it means that you'll have to trust me with your life." She said. Rowan stared at the supposed ground underneath him, if there was any at all.

"Well choosing between that," he said, indicating the no-floor under him, "and the mage who almost killed Carl, I think I'll pick you."

"Great. But this is going to be very risky. You'll have to let go if you want this to work. Take that sword out and throw it to me, and I'll climb up and get Solfang. I'm only about five feet below the ground, and I think I can make it." she said. But after a moment she added, "But you are almost certainly going to die."

"Then it wasn't much of a choice between you and the ground." Rowan said matter-of-factly. "Let's do it," He yanked the sword out of the stone wall and threw it as hard as he could. It flew over her head, but she managed to catch it before it went too far up, by the blade. Pain flared through her palm and fingers, but she had no time to lose. Rowan was already almost out of sight from where Cleo was now, and she had no idea how far down this hole went.

Cleo flipped the sword around and dug the blade into the stone, taking the other one out and stabbing it in again. She made it to the edge in a matter of seconds, but didn't stop to take her swords out of the wall. She pulled herself up and ran to Arella, who had all the animals in her necklace. But Cleo remembered her saying something to the pendant to release them.

"Release!" she said when she reached Arella. Nothing happened. "Out!" she tried. "Shelena!" she said, knowing that that was the spell to unleash something. The pendant wiggled as if responding to the spell, but quickly settled back down. It was probably enchanted to resist other spells in case there was something worth protecting in there.

This was not working. Rowan was probably already dead at the bottom of the hole. Cleo took a hold of the pendant and yanked it off the chain, which snapped in half and fell to the floor. The pendant, however, was still perfectly intact. Cleo threw it to the ground and smashed it with the heel of her boot. It shattered, releasing all the animals.

Cleo wasted no time in climbing on Solfang, who was luckily right next to her now, and pressing his horns forward. He dove into the hole with blazing speed and caught up to Rowan in no time. As she tried to grab him, one of his flailing arms slapped her in the face and almost knocked her off of Solfang's back.

She punched him back and grabbed his arm and flung him onto the dragon's back. Solfang swerved up, and all three were safely on the ground within moments. Cleo took both her swords out from the edge of the pit and resheathed them.

Cleo saw Tamsyn get too close to the rose on the pedestal. The floor underneath her collapsed as it had with Cleo. Solfang snarled and dove into that hole, too. A few seconds later he emerged with Tamsyn dangling from his claws. She was clutching her head like she was having a massive headache.

"What happened?" She moaned.

"A rose hypnotized you," Cleo said. The look of shock on Tamsyn's face was satisfying, but Cleo's smile faded when she turned to look back at the rose.

Solfang dropped her and Cleo leaped forward. She tugged Tamsyn's cloak over her eyes.

"Don't look at it!" she shrieked.

"Alright, alright!" Tamsyn's muffled voice said from under her cloak. Cleo got up and Tamsyn scrambled to her feet, cloak still over her head. Cleo covered her eyes and walked toward the rose. It wasn't hard finding it, even in a large room with her eyes closed. It gave off this aura which told her exactly where it was.

She opened her eyes one time to leap over the hole in the ground. Falling in again would not be fun.

A few moments later she was in front of the rose. She drew one of her swords and smashed the glass case to pieces. All of a sudden a terrible smell flooded her nose. It was so sudden and strong that she fell over with a yelp.

Cleo covered her nose and looked back. The others were doing the same. Others meaning Carl and Arella and Aiden and Ezra as well as Rowan and Tamsyn. The animals and Solfang were having a hard time covering their noses, especially Carl's wolf, who probably had a better sense of smell than everyone else, even Solfang.

Cleo grabbed the withering rose(it had no thorns) and held it away at arm's length. But as soon as she took it off of the pedestal, the blue light around the room faded and they entered pitch darkness.

CHAPTER 22

A shriek came from someone in the room. At first Cleo thought it was Ezra's leopard snarling, then she realized it was Carl.

Cleo held out her hand palm up as if she were holding something round and a little ball of fire appeared in it.

"That's so much better," she said.

"No it's not," Arella said. "Look."

Cleo looked down. Sure enough, millions of creepy small things were creeping through the cracks in the walls. Carl's wolf—Conri— and Rowan's lion had natural bug phobia, and were jumping around and barking and snarling. Tamsyn had a horse, a black one, but horses were mostly used to bugs and flies and had a very useful killing machine—their tail.

Solfang started hovering, with Carl's silly wolf holding onto his back, whining. Ezra's leopard, with its icy blue eyes, was surprisingly calm. It sat down majestically with its tail curled over its front paws. When the bugs came its way, they parted and curved around him.

Unfortunately for the others, no one else was as scary as the clouded leopard, and everyone was trying to get away from them. Cleo took a sip of the levitating potion from her tool belt.

"Hey, that's not fair!" Aiden said from the other side of the room. "You get to float?" Then he looked around. He was the only human left on the ground. Arella and Ezra were riding on Selkath, Cleo was floating, Rowan was with Carl and Tamsyn on Solfang. "Are you kidding me?"

Cleo groaned and tossed Aiden the vial. He took a sip and tossed it back to her, and she slipped it back into its loop on her belt.

But then a bigger problem arose. Cleo heard a creak in the walls that sounded like stone scraping. Then she heard water. But not the trickling leak in the ceiling, more like a rushing waterfall.

Cleo held her fire hand up and saw that there were now holes in the wall about the size of her head, and indeed, water was gushing out. It was unbearably loud, Cleo's ears felt like they were about to burst.

But that was the least of her problems.

Water was filling the room, fast, and Cleo guessed they only had a few minutes before the entire room was filled. And as it turned out, the bugs were water striders, which did not at all help with Ayala and Conri's bug phobia.

She glided to the pedestal where the rose had been moments ago. She placed the rose back where it was, and some of its petals grew back. It began to glow again, but the water didn't stop, so she picked it up again.

Cleo frantically scanned the room, looking for an exit, but the only openings in the big room were the tiny slits in the walls which the bugs had come through.

That gave her an idea, but it was risky.

"Wait here! I'll be back!" she yelled to the others at top volume. The people closest to her, Aiden, Arella, and Ezra, had heard here and were giving her quizzical looks. The others hadn't heard a thing.

Cleo floated to the nearest wall and used a shapeshifting spell to turn into a bug. She squeezed into the cracks. As a bug, she had pixelated vision, but she could have sworn there was a thin light at the end of the crack she was in. She scuttled as fast as she could to it and climbed out into an enormous cavern.

But as soon as she did, she regretted it. Just outside the room were the five slumbering sources of evil.

And just behind them, was the great mage Arcanum.

CHAPTER 23

Cleo couldn't believe it. She would have screamed if she were in human form.

Arcanum! Here! Now!

Cleo took a good pixelated look at what was in front of her.

The five Sources of Evil were sleeping in front of her. They looked like they were melting, which they probably were. Behind them was a huge woman, more or less.

The lower half of her body was sitting cross legged, with a wicked looking curved blade in her lap. It looked like it was made of bone. The upper half of her body, on the other hand, was nowhere to be seen.

It was clear that the five Sources of Evil were becoming the Black Sword, and fast.

Now to add on to the bad luck, Arcanum happened to be on the other side of the Sources, which was terrible, since they would sense her for sure and wake up if she tried to cross.

But on the bright side, Cleo was a bug, which was the most unsuspecting thing anyone could turn into. Unfortunately though, she wasn't very fast.

Her friends were counting on her, and were going to die in a few minutes if she didn't find a way to get them out. She had originally thought that there would be some hidden mechanism that could stop the water, but the universe just *had* to make her life difficult, so now she only had two options.

She could turn everyone into bugs and they all could make it out alive. Then they would all be safe and they could take down the Black Sword together. But the amount of magic it would take to turn six people into bugs would probably be enough to wake the Sources up, and then they'd have no time to wake up Arcanum.

On the other hand, if she made it to Arcanum now and woke him up, then she could ask him to get her friends out *and* they would have an ally when the

Sources sensed the magic and woke up. There were a few problems here, too. If the others were still alive by the time she got to Arcanum, they probably wouldn't be by the time she got him to wake up. And she also needed to wake him up without waking the Sources, too. But if things went well and somehow she made it back in one piece, then the result outweighed the risk.

Cleo went with the second option, but doubling back was a solid plan B.

She morphed into a dragonfly, which didn't take much magic, but she still saw one of the Sources stir and the Black Sword grip the handle of her weapon.

She winced and started flying as fast as she could to Arcanum, who was at least a half mile away from where she was now.

Either dragonflies were a lot faster than she remembered, or the universe was atoning for its wrongdoings, but before she knew it she was at the foot of Arcanum's bed.

It was a lot taller from here, so she turned back into her human form. She noticed that she still looked like Cleo, which was peculiar since she should have turned back into her real form—Eradoa. That was why she'd tried to avoid shape-shifting in front of the others, well, except Arella. But this was something to contemplate later.

Cleo now realized that shape-shifting back had been a mistake. Not only had she caught the attention of the Sources again, but because now she had to climb Arcanum's bed. More magic would be risky, though, and getting skewered by her supposed worst enemy before eve;waking the mage would probably not be the most heroic death.

It felt like eons had passed before she finally made it to the top of Arcanum's bed. It was quite large, as it was about ten feet above the ground. That may not seem like much to climb, but if you're particularly bad at climbing on a smooth golden surface without two helpful curved swords, then yes, it takes forever. The fact that Cleo's levitation potion was almost empty didn't help either.

When Cleo finally reached the top, she found Arcanum lying Snow White style in a velvet bed covered by a glass case. He looked impossibly old, with wrinkles covering his whole face, and a gray and white beard that stretched all the way to his waist. He looked congested, like he was eating a mixture of sauerkraut and fermented pickled fish while having the wildest dreams.

Cleo had no idea how to wake him without making any noise, and the glass case wasn't helping. The only way to get through it would be to shatter it. Even worse, her friends were probably a pile of drowned corpses by now.

Cleo thought hard. There had to be *something* she could do.

And then it hit her.

Cleo stared down at the smelly rose in her hands. If the glass shattered after Arcanum woke up, then it wouldn't matter because she wouldn't have to fight the Sources alone.

Cleo held the rose as close as she could to Arcanum's case. His nose twitched. Then twitched again.

The very next moment, he shot up.

"Monkey feathers!" he exclaimed at almost full volume, shattering the glass case. Cleo winced and clutched her ears, almost falling off the bed.

"Sorry," Arcanum said. This time Cleo yelped and actually fell off, landing with a heavy thud on the stone floor below.

"Ow," she groaned. Arcanum apologized once more and jumped down.

"What happened? What are the Sources doing here?" He said. Cleo blinked.

"Great!" she said. "You're awake! Nice to meet you Arcanum sir, now I really need your help."

Arcanum had the expression of a concussed sheep in an arena.

"Huh? Already?"

"You're a great mage. Please save my friends."

"Wait, what?"

Cleo was getting annoyed.

"Your magic? You can stop the water. Please?" His face twisted into all sorts of emotions.

"You're making no sense right now. Please slow down." He said.

"Okay. Let me start at the beginning." She said. "My name is Cleo. Me and my team killed the Cove Guardian, killed the snake queen Hemera, almost got killed, went through a portal to try and find you, but we got trapped in a room. I turned into a bug and found you, but my friends are still in that room. They're about to drown now, and I need you to save them, because I have no idea what to do. I've tried everything."

Arcanum stared at her with wide unblinking eyes.

Cleo guessed about five action-and-stressed-packed minutes had passed since she wiggled through the cracks in the walls, which was more than enough time for the room to completely fill up. Arcanum's hesitation was unbearable.

"Take me to these friends of yours. I'll see what I can do." He said after what seemed to be an eternity.

Cleo let out a breath that she didn't even know she was holding. She was about to turn back into a dragonfly when a voice behind her said,

"You're not going anywhere."

Cleo turned around to see the five Sources of Evil.

And they were all staring at her.

CHAPTER 24

Cleo would have screamed if she could get her voice to work. Of all the monsters, creatures, and ferocious beasts she had faced in her life, nothing scared her like this.

The five Sources had taken the form of black horses made of smoke. They were *really* big, about twenty times her own height, but were definitely smaller than Queen Hemera. They had dull pink eyes, and while pink was usually a cheerful color, that didn't make the Sources any less terrifying.

"Oh, Arcanum's here, too? What a wonderful reunion this is going to be." The voice said. It actually wasn't *a* voice, it was more like five voices speaking at the same time, hissing like a snake.

"Yes, I'm awake. After *you* put me to sleep." Arcanum said with sudden ferocity. There seemed to be more to this story than met the eye. "You, go." He said to Cleo, handing her a tiny silver sphere. "This will teleport you and your friends to me when it breaks. Now get out of here."

Cleo was about to shapeshift and leave, but hesitated.

"What about you?" she asked, finding her voice.

"I can take these turkey brains on my own for long enough. They can't kill me. Also, it's not the first time. Now get out of here before I have to worry about you."

Cleo nodded, turned into an eagle, and took off the way she came.

A few seconds later, she reached the wall from which she had crawled out of earlier. She risked a glance back, where she saw Arcanum with glowing white eyes battling the Sources. She turned back into a bug and wriggled back into the room.

But she was horrified to see that her worst nightmare had come true.

The water had reached the ceiling and the others were pinching their noses and holding their breaths. But that wasn't the worst part.

Carl, Aiden, and Arella, were all unconscious at the bottom of the room, bubbles coming out of their mouths. Tamsyn and Rowan weren't doing much better, judging by their red faces and swollen eyes.

Cleo turned back into a human and smashed the sphere against the wall as hard as she could. In a moment, three almost-dead people and three actually dead people came plopping down onto the great Archmage Arcanum's head.

"This is not what I had in mind when I conducted a daring rescue." Arcanum said from underneath six teenagers. "I thought there would be less skull crushing."

This seemed to wake everyone up, as both Arella and Aiden woke up, spitting water out of their mouths and gasping. They spotted Arcanum and hastily got onto one knee, bowing. Carl was still unconscious.

"Hello, fellow heroes. Now if you'll excuse me, I am in a battle here. And I could use some assistance." Arcanum said. Arella and Aiden scrambled onto their feet and performed a hasty salute. Then they noticed the Sources and yelped, falling back down.

"I never expected such noodle heads to make it all the way here. How in the third world did you get past the cove guardian?" the Sources said in unison. Cleo gritted her teeth.

At that moment, Carl woke up, vomiting water all over the ground. He saw the Sources and promptly fainted again.

"Alright, this is starting to bore me." The Sources hissed. "I'll just kill you all. See you in the afterlife."

Then they attacked.

CHAPTER 25

Two of the Sources lunged at Carl, knowing that he was the easiest target. Cleo pulled him out of the way right before smoky hooves smashed down on his face. The other three Sources lay back down and began melting into the Black Sword again. A glowing blue and red force field dome rose over them, which made taking them down ten times as hard.

Cleo took the invisibility potion out of her tool belt and shoved a few sips down his throat. He faded away, and Cleo threw him onto Solfang's back. She had to hope that Solfang could get him away fast enough before the Sources hit again.

Everyone except Cleo charged at the two Sources with their swords raised. Even though the enemy was outnumbered, Rowan and everyone else were outmatched.

Rowan aimed to slice off one of the smoke horses' heads, but his blade went clean through its head without doing any damage and slammed into Tamsyn's chest, scraping her armor. As it turned out, they could fade out at will and make things go through them. She had been sitting on one of the horses' backs trying to drive a dagger into its back, which seemed to be as hard as rock when it wasn't faded out. Even though Cleo had no idea how she did it, she was now sprawled on the floor thanks to Rowan's accidental blow.

At that moment Solfang came flying back. Cleo held one arm up and Solfang grabbed it with his front talons, flinging her onto his back. He flew over the Sources while spraying them with fire, careful not to hit any of the others. The fire seemed to have no effect on them, even though light was supposed to counter the darkness.

Cleo steered Solfang around and they flew in the other direction. She had an idea. And Tamsyn was her inspiration.

Solfang seemed to know what her plan was before she told him. He was already flying towards the

Sources again, but he swooped up and started spiraling higher and higher, until he was high enough for Cleo to put her plan into action.

The very next second Solfang turned around and started diving back to the ground, tucking his wings in to gain speed. Cleo was holding on tight to the edge of his saddle, the very thing she used to propel herself forward in the next moment. As soon as she was far enough away from Solfang, the dragon spread his wings fast and caught the air, gliding away to safety, leaving the rest of Cleo's plan up to her.

Cleo drew one of her swords in midair and twisted herself upright, bracing for impact. With luck, she would catch the horse by surprise and it wouldn't make her go right through it.

She planted her feet onto one of the smoke horses and used her momentum to drive her sword into its back. It screamed in pain, and twisted its head to see a new Excalibur stuck into its stone-hard hide.

It reared up and threw her off and she smashed into a stalactite, breaking it and possibly one of her rib bones into pieces. She flew into another one, this time stopping and sliding off. None of her friends had noticed her, they were still intent on winning the battle. Cleo sighed in relief, the last thing she needed was them getting distracted, only to end up like her.

Cleo tried to stand up, but her chest ached in protest. She grabbed onto a stalagmite and pulled herself up, leaning on it for support.

Cleo couldn't fight like this. She would just get herself killed.

She fumbled in her neverending pouches on the sides of her tool belt, searching for anything she could have saved before.

And then she found something. It was an old piece of cake that Elrod had enchanted and given to her and some of his other students back when she was still in mage training. It was supposed to heal any spells that could have caused serious damage.

Cleo had no idea whether it would work on broken bones. After all, when she had gotten it it was a full slice of cake that was newly enchanted. Now it was reduced to a single bite, a moldy one, too.

It looked the least bit appetizing, but she plugged her nose and shoved it down her throat, shuddering.

Less than two seconds later, she felt as good as new. She rushed back into the battle, feeling pumped and angry.

One of the Sources sent a ball of pure black magic at her, which she easily dodged. More came, and she jumped out of the way of each one. Until one hit her, and sent her flying back again. This time, she righted herself in midair and landed on two feet, skidding back several feet.

Cleo stood up straight and said a spell to herself. The soles of her boots started to glow, and so did her fingers. A light blue disk in the shape of a diamond appeared under her feet and lifted her a few inches off the ground. She thrust her hands back and she started skating across the stone floor to the fight.

As more balls of black magic came her way, she was able to dodge them more easily. Before she knew it, she was back in the midst of the battle. More dark balls of black stuff came her way, but she glided onto the walls, skating across the sides. She did a full circle around the inside of the cavern before returning to the ground and pulling out her shield.

She jumped off her skating disk and it disintegrated, like it was slowly turning into sand and blown away. Cleo's hands and feet turned back to normal, which was kinda sad because the glowing had actually looked pretty cool.

Cleo brought her shield in front of her, deflecting the occasional dark energy ball. She eyed the battle, wondering where she could slip in and possibly end one of the Sources.

But of course, her luck wasn't improving. It seemed that while she was enjoying a moldy bite of healing cake, another one of the Sources had joined the fight. It was hard to tell them apart, except for the one with Cleo's sword in its back. But singling out one of the others to attack would be hard.

Cleo was thinking about how to take even one of them down, when she was almost pulverized by one of the sources while she was distracted. Deciding that thinking was overrated, she rushed into the fight with no clear plan and was sent flying back for the third time almost immediately.

Alright. She was going to need a lot more than brute strength.

But now that she stopped to form a plan, one came to her almost immediately. More like two plans.

One, she could charge in and try to attack their hearts. If she looked closely, there was a small, faded red bulb that throbbed in the middle of the horses' chests, but getting to them would be nearly impossible since any attacks from the front would be seen and easily defended. She'd have to trick them into going fading out so she could walk through.

Two, she could attack from behind, using her friends as a distraction. But her timing would have to be spot on, or there would be consequences. Also, the Sources moved *fast*. Staying behind them and getting close would be a challenge for even a skilled warrior like her.

But then a third plan hit her. If she stayed on the ground, she'd be easy to spot, even if she was behind them. But if she came from above again, she could get onto the vulnerable horse's back and find a way to control it. And if she did the same thing twice, the horse wouldn't expect it. But she had to move *fast*.

She braced herself and whistled for Solfang.

CHAPTER 26

Cleo chose the weakest smoke horse to lay her plan on—the one with her sword lodged in its back. It was still dangerous, but it was in pain, too, making it the easiest target.

Solfang hovered over her head, ready for anything.

Cleo climbed the nearest stalagmite to get a better view of the fight. The Sources in their horse forms were huge, powerful, nearly invulnerable. It was hard to believe Rowan, Arella, Tamsyn, Aiden, unconscious Carl, Ezra, and Cleo were even a match for them.

Rowan and Tamsyn were teaming to take down the biggest of the Sources, the one that had been in the middle of them all when they were still sleeping. Tamsyn was incredibly agile, though each of her blows with her arms' length dagger seemed to simply annoy the horse. She easily dodged and flipped by the attacks with unnatural speed. While she drew the Source's attention, Rowan attacked its unguarded areas, once even getting dangerously close to its eye. But even together, with a mix of agility and strength, the Source seemed to barely be trying.

Arella and Aiden were attacking the second smoke horse, a slightly smaller one. Arella was blasting fire and wind from one hand while swinging her sword with the other, dealing significant damage to the Source. Her fire seemed to be hotter than Solfang's, as it burned holes through the smoke that made the horse's body. But each wound closed more quickly than it had formed. The horse bit and stomped at them, each crash of its hooves sending earthquakes quivering through the ground. And as it turned out, they could breathe fire, too. And also had laser eyes. And could stomp lightning. And could spew poison. Talk about overpowered.

While the heroes battled the Sources that were awake, Arcanum focused on breaking through the force field that covered the other two Sources, the ones that were sleeping and turning into the Black Sword. He occasionally turned around and delivered a blast of blinding white light that slammed into their sides and was enough to send them stumbling a few steps. Arcanum had his own force field around himself, as well as one encompassing every hero fighting. Cleo guessed that was the only reason they'd managed to stay alive through the earthquakes and the lightning and the lasers and the poison and the stomping hooves and the friendly fire.

Cleo knew things were already going bad, but wondered what would happen if the other two sources woke up. She'd guessed that the Sources intended to kill them first and then continue melting, mainly because the heroes had Arcanum on their side, who was the only one who could possibly break through the force field and stop them.

Cleo stopped thinking about the future. She alone would have to take down the third Source, and after she did, she would help Arcanum break through the force field around the other two that were melting.

Cleo gestured to Solfang above her. She jumped off her stalagmite and caught onto his horns, swinging herself onto his back.

"Get me above that one," she told Solfang, pointing at the third Source, the one with her sword lodged at the base of its neck. "Then get out of there. The next few minutes are going to be rough." Solfang snarled in response and flew fast dead ahead.

Cleo crouched on Solfang's back and crawled to the base of his long tail. As soon as she was right above her target, she dropped off. She and Solfang hadn't made a sound, and the Source had its back turned. There was no way it could possibly see or hear them from where it was.

She fell closer to the Source's back, but it didn't fall for her trick twice as she thought it would have. Just as she got into its range, it threw its head back and breathed a wall of flames at her. She had no idea this would happen.

"Nice try," it laughed as the flames got closer. Cleo didn't know what to do. She had only seconds. She screamed a wind spell, but nothing came out of her palms. The Source was grinning smugly at her. Had it somehow blocked her magic?

She should have thought of an escape plan. She was *so sure* her plan would have worked.

The heat was unbearable before she even touched the fire. She squeezed her eyes shut and threw her hands in front of her face, though it would have done nothing.

No, was the last thing she thought before she hit the walls of flames.

CHAPTER 27

Cleo knew she was going to get toasted. So why was it so cold? She felt like smooth marbles were rubbing against her face when she opened her eyes. At first she thought this was the afterlife. Warm light entered through the edges of her vision, and cool wind whistled in her ears.

Then she realized that she was concealed in something. Sheets of red were wrapped around her, and she recognized them as scales. *Solfang's* scales. It took a moment for Cleo to figure out what was going on.

Solfang must have shielded her when the fire came her way. But— Solfang didn't have fireproof scales. Other, more powerful species did, but not him. Then she smelled something burning.

Cleo squeezed herself out of Solfang's wings and screamed.

Solfang had been hit.

His scales had turned from dark red to almost black. Some of the fire was still alive on his back and along his tail. Both him and Cleo were falling.

She slapped his snout and yelled into his ear to wake up. When he didn't, nightmare possibilities flashed through her mind. Was he dead? Did the Source kill him? If Solfang was dead, she was going to rip the Sources apart and crush their hearts with her bare hands. She would paint the walls of this cavern with their blood.

Then she realized she was still quite a distance above the third Source. The fire had blasted them upward, almost all the way to the cavern's ceiling. She could still go through with her plan.

Finally, after lots of yelling and slapping, Cleo decided to splash water in his face with a spell. Solfang woke up with a start and righted himself. He spread his charred wings to break his fall and started gliding. He groaned and growled as he glided away.

Cleo gave him one final pat on the back and jumped off. The Source obviously thought she was a pile of ashes, because it didn't expect what she was going to do next. It was busy trying to catch Tamsyn when she landed on its back.

"Erif Orfini," she said, and a huge ball of fire the size of her face ignited in her hand. She clenched her fist and flicked her arm out. The fireball extended into a rope of flames and she whipped it around the Source's head. It wound around its muzzle and neck like a bridle and reins made of fire.

It reared up and thrashed around, trying to buck her off. It certainly was not easy riding a horse fifty times her size. She'd never even ridden a regular horse before.

Cleo had to admit that she didn't think this plan was going to work. It took all of her focus and concentration to keep the flames alive and hang on tight to the horse's body at the same time. She had one hand controlling the fire and the other hand firmly gripping the handle of her sword that was conveniently embedded at the base of its neck between the horse's shoulder blades. But even so, she was hanging on for dear life.

Cleo pulled as hard as she could on the reins of fire. The Source made a bloodcurdling noise that sounded like a cross between a neigh and a snake's hiss as the flames around its muzzle tightened and sunk into the smoky flesh. Cleo kicked as hard as she could on the sides of the Source's body, but she doubted it felt a thing.

It started running forward really fast, attempting to throw her off. She loosened her grip on the reins, and the Source started running faster, just like she'd counted on it doing.

"Nice work, Cleo!" She heard Rowan call as she passed the other Sources.

As she did, Cleo pulled the reins to the right and rammed the Source into the other Sources. She was careful not to hit any of her friends, though. The Source she was riding wasn't as big as the others, but with its momentum, it packed a serious punch when rammed into stuff.

The Source skidded to a halt and turned to the left to avoid hitting the cavern walls, but didn't stop running, bucking and thrashing all the way. Cleo yanked on the reins and bashed it into the wall to its right, hard enough for the rock to crack. The Source staggered, but didn't slow down.

Suddenly, the Source changed course and turned slightly to the left. It was headed towards a garden of stalagmites.

Cleo wasn't prepared for what was going to happen next. But then again, she was hardly ever prepared for anything. The Source was running towards a tall rock spire in the ground. She tried steering it away, but it persisted and didn't turn, though it whinnied and roared in pain as the fire burned through its smoky body.

The Source was right next to the spire when it rammed its side against it. Cleo's leg was caught between the Source and the rock, and it was smashed with a sickening *crunch*.

Cleo screamed.

She let go of the fire reins and flames died down. She toppled off the Source's back and fell onto her side, rolling multiple feet back and leaving trails of dust behind her.

The Source kept running. It was a good distance away from her when it doubled back and went straight for her.

Lying on the floor with a broken leg and no dragon to rescue her, Cleo knew for a fact that there was no saving her life now.

In a few moments, for real this time, she was going to die.

CHAPTER 28

First there was wind. Then there was fire.

Then there was a mysterious invisible force running around and making a lot of noise.

Then there was a pair of flying toes.

Then the unexpected happened.

The Source was running at top speed at her with fire in its pink eyes. It seemed to have gotten bigger and stronger, but that was maybe because Cleo's fear had gotten bigger and stronger as well.

But out of nowhere it slipped and was knocked to the side, just seconds away from trampling her. It was as though a giant hammer had slammed into its side.

Cleo was in too much pain to care about what was happening. Then she realized that someone was rubbing her broken leg.

She looked up and found Ezra wrapping something that looked like a wooden boot around her leg. She looked even higher up and saw the invisible force single handedly battling the third Source. Suddenly, the figure faded into view. Cleo gasped.

It was Carl.

He was awake.

And he was taking on the Source of Evil by himself.

Cleo watched as Carl battered and beated the Source with brute strength. Then she realized, with a start, that the strength potion from her tool belt was empty next to her. Huh.

A few seconds later, he appeared on top of the Source's head with a long string in his hands.

"You know, Cleo," he called, smiling down at her. "The fire was pretty impressive, but regular ropes work fine, too, you know?"

He flicked the rope he was carrying around the Source's head and slipped down onto its back.

Cleo would smile if she had the energy to.

Ezra pulled out a little green square that looked like leaves wrapped together and gave it to her.

"Eat this," he said. "It's called ambrula. It'll help."
She was in no condition to argue.

She opened her mouth and gobbled it down. It was then that she realized that she was quite hungry, too. All the battles and wild rodeos took up quite a lot of energy.

As soon as she swallowed the ambrula, the pain receded. Ezra stopped her from standing up right away, telling her that the ambrula only numbed the pain, but didn't completely heal the injury.

Cleo didn't want to sit out of the fight. She wanted to help. She decided to try out a spell she'd never done before.

She stood up on one leg and muttered a spell to herself. It took a lot of concentration and willpower, but soon enough, two large maroon dragon wings sprouted from her back. She'd never attempted this spell before, mainly because it took a lot of blood to perform it using blood magic.

"Can't stop a mage," she said, and took off.

She was about to get into the fight when she spotted Solfang lying on the ground with his eyes closed.

She was so engrossed with saving her own life that she'd completely forgotten about him.

Cleo's determined expression was replaced with worry as she swooped down and landed next to her old friend, who was sprawled on the ground with his wings spread out. He was hardly breathing, and when he did, his breaths were shaky and unsteady.

Cleo gasped when she took a closer look at his injuries. He was badly burned in many areas, especially his wings. Black lines spread like rivers across his charred back.

Cleo flipped him over onto his back to examine the areas that had been directly hit.

It was horrible.

Solfang had been scorched almost everywhere on his front side. His head and neck were fine, as it was instinctive to protect his face when he leapt in front of her.

But along his chest and underbelly and all the way to the base of his tail was a deep gash that was spilling gallons of blood. If he didn't die of his wounds, blood loss would be the second worst thing.

But that wasn't it.

His right arm had a cut that went down to the bone and another one on his thigh.

Cleo was so glad he was unconscious. Once he woke up, his burns were going to hurt a *lot*.

A tear fell from her eyes and landed on some of Solfang's smooth unburned scales. This was *her* fault. It was *her* plan, and *she* had dragged Solfang into it. It was *her* fault her dragon was dead.

At that moment, she didn't care if a smoke horse ran her over. She didn't care if everyone died because she wasn't in the fight anymore. She didn't care that darkness could take over the world. So much guilt was welled up in her chest that she couldn't think to care about anything.

Ezra ran over to her and Solfang. Cleo hardly even noticed him until he started treating Solfang's wounds.

"What are you doing?" she asked.

"I'm stopping the blood," he replied. He was dabbing a huge piece of cotton on Solfang's chest, soaking up any of the leaking blood.

"Why?" Cleo asked. It seemed pretty stupid to try and save a dead dragon. She told him this, but he simply shook his head.

"He's not dead. His blood hasn't clotted and his body is still warm." He didn't look up at her, but he smiled.

Cleo sucked in the tear that was about to fall.

"You, get back into that fight right now. Carl needs you. I got this." Ezra said. Cleo wanted to stay but got the hint that this was not under negotiation. And Carl, indeed, really did need help.

She took off and rejoined the battle, charging a small flame in her hand. Carl's strength was wearing off. The Source was too big for him to fight alone on the ground. It blasted lightning and poison and fire at him. The earthquakes made it nearly impossible to stand.

Cleo's wild riding had taken its toll on the third Source. It was wobbly and unsteady. She had done the hard part, now she and Carl just needed to finish it off.

She swooped down and thrust her hand forward, blasting a beam of fire at its back, the weak area that had been stabbed with her sword. It roared and tried to kick her out of the sky, but she swerved out of the way and attacked again.

Carl jumped onto the horse's back and tried to reach its heart through the parts of it that faded out.

She kept diving and blasting until the third Source was on its knees.

She angled her wings up and hovered right above its head, igniting a red ball of fire in the palm of her hand. She tightened the muscles in her entire arm and it condensed into a white-hot ball of pure heat and energy. Her hand flew forward and the flame extended into a supernova of light and fire.

This time the Source didn't scream. It didn't roar, whinny, or hiss either.

Its horse form disintegrated and reduced to a flying plume of smoke no bigger than Cleo's head.

Cleo knew they couldn't really kill any of the sources. Good couldn't live without Evil as its counterpart. So she held out her hand and clenched it into a fist. Loose stalactites broke down into pebbles and floated to her. She flicked out her four last fingers and the rocks flew at the Source and smashed it to the ground. She curled her fingers in slowly one by one and hardened the rocks into a strong cage around the Source, trapping it in one place. But just in case, she added a protection spell, reinforcing it with light magic.

Carl looked up at her. He had jumped off when she hit the Source with the supernova spell.

"Seriously, you keep finding all sorts of crazy ways to fly. I mean, who has a levitation potion, rides a dragon, and grows wings all in one lifetime?" He complained, grinning. Cleo laughed for the first time in forever.

"Come on, pea brain. We've got to help them." She said and flew off to the others. She had a plan to take the other Sources out, but it would be exhausting and would leave her vulnerable for a solid few minutes.

She made her way to the force field. Arcanum had seared open a small hole, big enough for him to poke his arms into. He was now trying to rip the rest open.

"Archmage!" she called. "I need your help!" She landed on one foot next to him and explained her plan in as few words as possible.

"That's risky, but it might work," he said. "Let's do it."

CHAPTER 29

Cleo flew ahead. Her plan required her to get directly above the two remaining Sources. She dodged blasts of fire and lightning and whipping tails and accidental friendly fire. Then one of the Sources noticed her. It reared up and snapped its teeth, which were wicked sharp.

Cleo swerved around its head and shot forward as fast as she could. It dodged and threw a row of flames at her.

"Not this time," she muttered, and countered it with a shield of wind. The other Source now spotted her, and singling her out as an easy target, it spat poison and lightning in her direction. The other one did the same. She hardly had any reaction time, but remembered she had magic, too. She set her arms out and the poison circled around her, the lightning crackling and bending. Both disappeared only a moment later.

She looked down at Arcanum and nodded. His fists blazed with fire, propelling him upward at blinding speed. Cleo retreated to the ground next to her friends.

Arcanum fought his way to the place above both Sources. This was the part that left him unguarded and very vulnerable.

"Nogard inferno," he shouted, and a tiny sprout of fire appeared in his hand. At that moment, Cleo held out her hands and waved them horizontally like she was spreading invisible jelly on a huge loaf of bread. Instantly a wave of pink and light blue washed over Cleo and Solfang and the rest of her friends and the animals to protect them from Arcanum's crazy spell. The archmage had taught the spell to Cleo himself. It was the only one that could withstand his magic.

The Sources could only watch as the sprout of fire started to grow. It kept growing and growing until it was the size of the average fat person. Arcanum held it above his head and it kept growing.

Two seconds later, it went supernova and combusted. Blinding golden light engulfed the Sources. Naturally, Arcanum was immune to the effects of his own spell, and the force-field around Cleo and her friends protected them.

The light died down a little and Cleo watched in pleasure as the light burned the two other Sources away—the more powerful ones. The force field around the other two Sources protected them, but that didn't matter as of now.

As soon as the spell faded, everyone else opened their eyes. The two incinerated Sources were there on the ground, wiggling and flying around in their new and improved tiny forms. Cleo had to admit, they were kind of cute when they weren't trying to kill her.

Cleo whipped up two more rock cages and trapped the two Sources.

Then they entered a phase of awkward silence.

For a few solid seconds they stood there, not knowing what to say. They'd just won a battle by the skin of their teeth. Cleo looked around and saw that everyone's pale skin, and even Tamsyn's dark brown skin, had turned almost completely red from bleeding gashes and wounds.

Aside from herself, Cleo noticed both Carl and Arella were limping. Aiden had a huge chunk of flesh taken out from one side, and it was bleeding like crazy. Ezra had no fresh wounds, but he was scratched and beaten up from fighting and treating wounds at the same time. Rowan wasn't too badly hurt, but he was bleeding from a thousand cuts almost everywhere and there was a nasty line of blood dripping from his hairline as if he had cracked his skull with a hatchet.

Cleo was still flying, which made her look better than she really was, but she had a broken leg and her arms were sliced up. She couldn't see it, but she felt a long bleeding cut going down her back, soaking the tunic she was wearing under her armor, which, too, had been split open down the middle. And despite being saved by Solfang, her entire body was still smoking from the third Source's fire attack, and any exposed skin had been charred and burned.

Cleo landed and hobbled over to Solfang, who was still being treated by Ezra. He looked a lot better, mainly because he was awake now. Though the bleeding had been stopped, he was wrapped in so many red blood-soaked bandages that he almost looked normal again.

Cleo was happy he was alive. She didn't know how she would live with herself if Solfang had died trying to save her. She sat down next to him and rested her head on his neck, one of the only parts of him that hadn't been damaged. She closed her eyes and drifted into an uneasy sleep. The last thing she saw was the others all laying down and closing their eyes as well.

.   .   .

Cleo awoke to the sound of thunder. The others were already awake. Then she realized what had happened.

She looked down at the floor. The cages with the three Sources in them were trembling, and the other two Sources were awake. The force field was gone, now, but nobody was trying to attack them, even though it was eight against two.

The two bigger Sources had created a mini thunderstorm above everyone, at least it *sounded* like a thunderstorm. There were dark clouds swirling up ahead like a vortex and small shoots of lighting were flickering here and there.

Cleo couldn't explain it, but it was exhilarating. She should have been terrified, or angry, or confused, but she was feeling something completely different, something like excitement or anticipation. It was creepy, like these emotions were being forced on her, not like they were something she actually felt.

The thunder got louder, and she saw everyone else cover their ears. She and the other Sources, however, stayed perfectly still and watched the clouds. Then she heard something else, something like smashing rocks, when she saw that the three tiny Sources had broken out of their cages, which were now crumbling pebbles. They flew up to the vortex, but halfway there they melted into blobs and elongated into thin swirling worm-like things. The three Sources melted into one another, fusing into one giant blob of black wispy smoke.

The bigger Sources, too, faded away like grains of sand and merged with the small blob in the center. They grew in size and started turning all sorts of different colors from black to dark purple.

Then two glowing pink eyes appeared in the middle.

"Thank you. You've done us a big favor." They said in a voice that sounded like a dragon mixed with a cow mixed with a snake.

Then the eyes vanished and the Sources started spinning. They slowly started to rise to the middle of the vortex and got harder and harder to see. They entered the storm and the thunder got louder than ever. Cleo crouched down and slammed her palms onto her ears.

Then, all of a sudden, the vortex disappeared and a plume of smoke rose out of what had been the center. It looped twice in the air before floating over to Cleo and the others.

"You have done us a great service," they hissed, and spiraled through the air over to the half Black Sword. The plume of smoke sunk into her body and the whole cavern started to shake.

The rest of the Black Sword appeared remarkably fast and she opened her eyes.

"Finally," she sneered. Her eyes were dark pink, just like the Sources in their horse forms.

Cleo and the others readied their weapons. Arcanum had an unreadable expression, but his whole body radiated hate and anger.

"Arcanum! Haven't seen you in so long! It's been almost three billion years since I put you to sleep, hasn't it, old friend?" the Black Sword mused. Arcanum growled and held his hand out next to him as if he were holding a staff. A moment later, a staff actually appeared in his hand. It was pure white and had an icy blue orb at the very top which was clasped in small branches of wood that extended from the stick of the staff. It didn't look imposing, but radiated a powerful aura.

"Nice to see you again too, *old friend*." Arcanum said sarcastically.

"Yeah yeah, whatever." The Black Sword said. She gazed over the other heroes and stood up, brandishing her blade, which was deep black—hence the name. Cleo felt uneasy looking at the sword. There was something wrong about it. Then she realized the blade didn't gleam or shine, not even reflecting the light coming from the dim glow of the cavern. It stayed pitch black, like an inky shadow.

"You've caused a lot of trouble." She said, "I thought you would be dead by the time you reached Queen Hemera. Very impressive, though." Arella clenched her hands into fists and put them in front of her, like she was getting ready for a martial arts battle. They burst into flames that reflected in the Black Sword's gleaming eyes.

But then the Black Sword's eyes set on Cleo. In them Cleo saw hatred, anger, power, greed. But all the emotions started swimming together when they saw her.

"What are you doing here?" she said blandly. Her tone had nothing to it, no manipulating tinge or hateful smirk. It was just...cold.

"I think I would remember seeing a four billion year old giant lady if I'd seen one before." She said, "Don't act like you know me."

"Oh but I *do* know you. I've been watching you since the beginning."

Cleo gulped. "Beginning of what?" The Black Sword chuckled.

"Oh, your father really didn't tell you? You and I go long back, longer than you remember."

"We do?" Cleo was shivering. The Black Sword grinned, but there was nothing fierce or threatening in the gesture. She crouched to one knee and lowered herself to Cleo's position.

"Oh, yes." She said. "I'm your mother."

CHAPTER 30

Cleo almost fell over. What?

No wonder her father refused to talk to her about her mother. No wonder Elrod was looking for her so desperately. And looking back at it, the leaders were always wary around her. It all made sense now.

The others were staring at her, but she couldn't make herself care. This was too much to take in at once.

Then she did the most impossible thing.

She dropped her swords. They clattered on the ground, but she didn't notice.

"How?" she breathed, barely managing it. "You've been asleep for billions of years."

"Well, I may have been sleeping, but I am still powerful enough to project myself to the real world every once in a while. Of course, I didn't have any power as a projected image, though." The Black Sword replied. "Which reminds me,"

233

She lifted her sword like she was poking something in the air, and the vortex appeared again.

"I'll need this," she said, the anger emerging in her eyes again. The whole cavern started to shake, and small black birds started flying out of the vortex. They looked like Selkath, except one fourth the size and numbering in the hundreds. They let out ear-piercing screeches that sent fear down Cleo's spine.

Selkath chirped angrily, unfolding his wings and crouched, his elegant features gleaming in the dim light of the cavern.

"Black Phoenixes," the Black Sword said. "Good luck dealing with these."

Cleo put on a determined expression and picked up her swords. Mother or no mother, this lady was going down today. She spread her wings and took off, the others running not far behind her. Now all they needed was a good theme song in the background.

The Black Sword hardly batted an eye. She swung the back of her black bone sword like a whip and tripped everyone. Well, almost everyone. Tamsyn and her inhuman reflexes jumped out of the way and landed on the sword, gripping the dull edge tightly. When the sword returned to the Black Sword, she climbed up the blade and the hilt and up the Black Sword's arm.

She was the size of a tarantula compared to the towering woman, but that hardly mattered. She made it all the way to the Black Sword's eye before being smacked off.

Cleo angled her wings and swooped down, her sword raised. She was caught by her good foot and flung back to where she came from.

"I'm not going to hurt you, Ery. All I ask is for you to stay out of the way while I finish off these nuisances." She heard the Black sword shout. All of a sudden, Cleo felt a longing to join her, which came out of nowhere. She knew her loyalties and wasn't going to let her past influence her future.

"My *name* is *Cleo!*" she yelled back, half to let her mother know, and half to remind herself.

"Yes, and you named yourself after me." The Black Sword said. She was right. Her real name was Cleone.

She spread her wings and held herself in the air before rushing again. But this time she tried a different approach. She took a sip of her invisibility potion—which was almost empty—and changed course to attack from behind. She held up an invisible hand and a lightning bolt appeared in it, crackling and flashing. She launched it at her mother with all her might.

It combusted in midair, breaking up into a bunch of smaller bolts that cracked and sizzled even louder. But as soon as they made contact with the Black Sword's armor, they exploded. The dust and smoke cleared after a minute. There was not a scratch on the smooth silver chestplate.

Cleo swooped up to avoid colliding with the Black Sword's rock-hard armor.

She drew one of her swords and threw it into her eye. She blinked and the sword clanked and bounced off.

"Seriously, Eradoa. Stop trying to kill me. It's not going to work." She said, rolling her eyes.

Cleo roared with anger and flew back as fast as she could. She would be invisible for a couple more hours, if she was lucky.

She charged again and again, blasting her mother with fire and lightning and metal and water and explosives and practically anything dangerous she could get her magical hands on. Nothing worked, obviously.

Cleo knew she couldn't win with melee and magic. She was playing good. Her mother was playing dirty. Every once in a while she would try and step on one of her friends, but Arcanum cast a temporary force field whenever that happened. He was the one who was dealing the most damage to the Black Sword while the others fought off the black phoenixes spilling out of the vortex. He blasted balls of what looked like pure white energy. They were enough to make the Black Sword stagger back a step, but did no visual damage.

Cleo's attacks, on the other hand, did almost nothing. Not a scratch, not a sign, not a clue of any pain on her mother's side. It was *really* annoying.

Cleo didn't know what to do, so she used the last thing she had at her disposal. Her brain. She'd faced the toughest of enemies, she had found her way through multiple precarious predicaments, and she'd literally ridden one of the five Sources of Evil. If she could get past those, she could get past this.

Cleo got up and spread her no longer invisible wings. Had it been two hours already? She took off, slicing up phoenixes and friendly fire and attacks. The Black Sword seemed to have noticed her, because blasts of fire, wind, and this weird glowing pink stuff came her way, she held her hands out and a red circular half-dome formed before her, deflecting attacks and protecting her from her evil mom. She also noticed that these attacks were significantly less damaging than the ones battering her friends.

She hovered in front of her mother's huge face, but she was far enough to notice any attack the moment one was fired. Many came her way, but she swiped them out of the way with the flick of a hand.

Now came the hard part.

If magic didn't work, then she would have to stoop down to a level she never thought she would need to.

Regular magic had no effect, but that was because the Black Sword was used to dealing with enemies on the other side of the power scale. To defeat her, she would have to be hit with something she didn't know how to defend.

Curses.

Cleo took a deep breath and prepared herself to use dark magic for the first time in a long time.

She pulled out one of her swords and sliced off her hand. A spell like this required a *huge* sacrifice.

To be quite honest, Cleo had no idea whether she would have the willpower to cut off her own hand, but she did.

Blood poured out of her wrist like a waterfall, splattering on the ground beneath her.

The pain was unbearable, but she didn't scream or cry. She kept her eyes on her mother, who was watching her with a ferocious gleam in her eyes.

"Now why would you need to do that?" she asked with sly curiosity.

Cleo ignored her and closed her eyes. A moment later she opened them, and they were pitch black. She held out her left arm, the one that had been hacked, and a new hand grew. She twisted her fingers and wrist. The light and matter around her hand seemed to bend and spiral towards the center of her palm as she curled her fingers in.

Her hand turned black. As soon as it was in a complete fist, the black grew over the rest of her body, until all other colors were overtaken. Cleo let out a breath and the blackness condensed and left her body, shooting at the Black Sword.

It collided with her chestplate and the blackness washed over her. Within a few seconds, she was completely encased in the blackness. She keeled over and fell onto one knee. She had stopped breathing, and was gasping for any air left in her lungs. Everyone was watching. Even the black phoenixes had stopped biting and scratching. For a moment, Cleo almost thought it had worked.

But then the Black Sword started laughing. A hysterical, amused laughter.

She got back up as the blackness shrunk until it was gone completely. Cleo had no idea what went wrong.

"Oh, deary. You can't hurt me with my own magic. Even though that is a very impressive spell. Well done, darling." She said. Anger welled in Cleo's chest. Magic wouldn't work and she couldn't use her swords either. Her sudden hate and anger drowned her logical and rational side and she felt heat rising up in her body. That was a bad sign. She forced herself to calm down. It wouldn't do anyone any good if she exploded herself with rage.

Cleo got an idea.

The problem was that she was using either magic *or* melee. But what if she used both?

She placed a hand on her sword and made it grow three times as big. It was heavier, too, but she didn't stop there. She charged it with a killing curse, a sleeping curse, a fire spell, a lightning spell, a freezing curse, a crushing curse, and a dragonbreath inferno spell. If this didn't work, nothing would. But she would need a diversion, again, for this to work.

She laid her eyes on Arcanum, who was shooting blasts of very powerful magic at the Black Sword's face. Each blast set her on fire temporarily, and seemed to be dealing lots of damage. Sometimes she even let out a small cry of pain, which was *really* something.

She landed on one foot next to him.

"Arcanum, I need to draw her attention. Give her everything you've got." She said. He nodded and started throwing a bunch of random spells at her. A beam of water, fire, and similar pink goo shot at her. He pointed his staff at the ground and then at the Black Sword, and three huge boulders came crashing into her chestplate with enough force to knock her back a few steps.

"Why weren't you fighting like this before?" Cleo asked. Arcanum was the only one whose power matched that of the Black Sword's, and he was going easy on her?

"Well, using magic like this is very tiring after sleeping for three billion years. I'd like to see *you* try it sometime." He countered.

"She doesn't seem to have a—,"

"Carry on with your master plan," he said, adding a touch of sarcasm to the *master plan* part. She scoffed, sipped her invisibility potion, and flew off with her ginormous sword and its million spells and curses.

She waited for a while until the battle was big enough to draw all the Black Sword's attention. The others had stopped battling the black phoenixes and were sending everything they had at the Black Sword. Cleo noticed Aiden sending a few blasts of magic at her. Arella must have taught him some of what she knew.

Cleo took a deep breath and sent all her power into her sword, both light and dark. It started to glow yellow with streaks of black down the middle that looked like rivers and tributaries, indicating that it was now as powerful as she could make it.

Cleo shot forward as fast as she could with her cursed sword and raised it high above her head. But as she flew, she heard a voice in the back of her mind that sounded like her, but older.

Give up. It rasped.

Stop fighting. She heard it say. She tried to ignore it, but it got louder as she neared the Black Sword.

Give in to the darkness.

Join me.

Betray your friends, they mean nothing to you.

Cleo felt a strange longing to do what it commanded, but she pulled herself together as she got closer to the Black Sword.

And once she was close enough, she swiped her sword as hard as she could (with her superstrength) at the Black Sword's neck, aiming for the killing blow.

But as soon as she made contact, the world around her turned pitch black.

CHAPTER 31

Give in.

Choose wisely.

Give up.

You're stronger than the others.

Give in.

GIVE IN.

The voice in Cleo's head was louder than ever, now. She couldn't see anything, even when she opened her eyes, but she could hear everything the voice said. She also felt weird, like her body had been melted and turned into a blob. She kept wiggling like she had been turned into smoke.

Give in.

Choose.

Your friends or the power?

Choose wisely.

Give in.

Cleo wanted to do as the voice said. Her friends were weak, and her mother was strong.

Two visions popped up in front of her. One was of her and her friends, who were racing together on their animals and laughing. But in the next moment, they were ambushed by monsters. They were greatly outnumbered, but they won the battle and moved on, only to find another battle waiting for them. Then another, and another, and another. By the end of it, everyone was beaten up and bloody. The vision seemed to go on forever, battle after battle after battle. Cleo had to pull herself out of it.

The other vision showed Cleo standing by her mother and laughing, but not as she had with her friends. This was a cackling kind of laughter. But what she was laughing *at* was even worse. Villages had been burned down. There were bloody corpses at her feet. Entire armies had been wiped out, and the whole world was burning.

She understood the meaning of both visions.

The voice was trying to get her to choose between being with her friends, only to almost die every day, or having all the power in the world and watching the world burn.

Cleo was even more horrified that this was a tough choice. She wanted to be with her friends more than ever, but the other choice was strangely appealing, like, *hypnotizingly* appealing. She reached her hand towards it and stepped into the vision.

But that was the worst mistake in her life.

She found herself in her mother's eye, viewing things like she would. She saw Arcanum sweating and fighting as hard as he could, every one of his blasts sending shivers down her body.

Cleo was doing things she didn't tell herself to do, like she had become someone she was not.

That was it!

Choosing the pain and torture path was the option to become her mother.

And that was the *last* thing Cleo wanted for herself.

But...it wasn't all that bad.

Will you join me? The extremely annoying raspy voice said again, but this time it sounded more like her mother instead of like her.

Cleo wanted to say no. She *really* wanted to say no. Her friends needed her right now. They were tired, and they were losing the battle. Not that they were winning earlier, though.

Cleo was about to say no, but something in the back of her head clicked. She was flooded with all the good memories she had with Elrod, all the sweet moments of beheading and finger slicing. Those were beautiful, and she missed being reckless and irrational and not having to think twice about *everything*.

But only a few days with the heroes had completely changed her point of view. She had real friends, allies. She trusted them with her life. They had to take down evil and stop the world from crumbling into darkness. This wasn't about her. It was about the world. Everyone was counting on her. She couldn't let this happen.

Say no to the pain, she thought.

Say no to the torture.

Say no to the dark future.

Say no. Say no. Say no.

Eradoa looked down through her mother's eyes and said, "Yes."

CHAPTER 32

It felt good to be back.

Eradoa missed her old self more than she realized. As much fun as it was being with Arella and the others, she was so much more *powerful* now. And power was better than anything else. Why have love when you could have *fear*?

She eyed her surroundings. Her leg was no longer broken, and she was standing on a tall rock ledge. Her mother was far off in the battle, and she doubted anyone could see her from where they were.

She still had those fake dragon wings she had whipped up. Very handy.

She flew to her mother and landed on the ground next to her. Eradoa didn't have a very good memory, but she was sure her mother had been a lot taller than this the last time she saw her.

"Mother, why is this battle still going on?" she asked with genuine curiosity.

"Oh, I was waiting for you to do the honors." Mother replied. Eradoa nodded and stepped forward with her hands blazing.

"Cleo, what happened to you?" Arella called from her Blue Phoenix above.

"Oh, I had a makeover," she said, not really thinking through how stupid that answer was. She had no time to be annoyed.

She inhaled and exhaled while slicing her hand and collecting her blood. She inhaled again, a little stronger now, and exhaled hard. A black transparent dome appeared around her, and she inhaled and exhaled again. Every time she took a breath, the dome got bigger, until she knew it was large enough to take care of everyone. She pulled her levitation potion out of her tool belt and splashed the rest of the vial onto the ground. It mixed with the dome and charged it with a levitation spell.

With one swift movement, she spun a 360 and slammed her hand onto the ground. It sent trembles through the ground and to the outer edges of the dome, which grew bigger really fast and popped.

Everyone in the dome except for Eradoa started to levitate. She controlled every muscle in their body (except for their brain) and floated them all to the vortex swirling above them.

But at that time Arella found the opportunity to try and strike her from above.

"Cleo, what are you doing?" she yelled and jumped off her phoenix, landing a few steps in front of Eradoa.

"You guys are too much trouble." she said. "And I'll need this." She yanked off Arella's pendant with ease and threw it up into the vortex. Selkath seemed to be attached to the pendant, and was thrown forward as well when it was sucked in.

"Selkath!" Arella shrieked. "Cleo, what happened to you?"

Eradoa smirked. This was the exact reaction she had been hoping for.

"Don't worry, Arella. They're alive." She said in the least reassuring way. "And you can go join them,"

Arella looked at the vortex and back at the ground.

"No," she said, readying her weapon.

"Oh? You want to fight me?" Eradoa looked up at her mother. "What should I do, mother? Should I fight her?" Then without waiting for an answer, she shook her head. "No." She flicked her hand and Arella went flying into the vortex along with her horrible friends.

Eradoa looked up at her mother.

"Are they actually alive in there?" she asked.

"Yes," Mother said. "But don't worry. They're in a place where we won't ever have to worry about them again. Now let's go kill something,"

Eradoa grinned and followed her mother into the real world.

This was going to be fun.

Epilogue

Arella woke up to find herself in a jungle. Her head hurt like she had been knocked out, but it didn't hurt as much as her heart did.

Cleo, Arella's best friend, had turned on her, choosing fear and power over strength and loyalty. And that was enough to make anyone go insane.

Arella rolled over onto her back, breathing hard. She felt like she'd been asleep for a century. Her vision was blurred, but she was sure there was someone looking down on her.

"Earth to Arella! Welcome back." They said. She didn't know who it was, but she took the hand that came down to her and pulled herself up.

"Who are you?" she asked.

"Come on, silly! Did you go blind or something?" They said, Arella looked around and her vision cleared a few seconds later. She looked back down.

"Oh, it's you." Tamsyn was standing in front of her.

"Yep. Rowan sent me to get you." She said cheerfully. Then a dark expression filled her face. "Follow me, we've got a problem."

Arella sighed and bounded after her friend. As her vision cleared further, she noticed that they were in a jungle. A really dense jungle with lots of sunlight and only a few open areas where they could see the sky.

A few minutes later they entered a clearing. Everyone else was there. She was happy to see them, but the worried looks on their faces ruined the reunion.

"Oh, good. You're here," Rowan said. He looked more anxious than usual.

"What happened?" she asked. "Are you alright?"

The others exchanged glances.

"Yes. We've been teleported to some weird place. I have no idea where we are." Rowan said. "Even Ezra doesn't know."

Arella looked over at Ezra, who was studying a huge scroll. His usually neatly combed hair was tousled and messy. His eyes were sunken in and dull, as if he hadn't slept in days. Next to him was a pile of maps, charts, and books, half of which were torn and dirty.

"We're not in a place that's on any of my maps. I guess we're in some kind of hidden place that nobody knows about, or it would have been *somewhere*."

"I guess that means this place is off the charts?" Carl offered. No one laughed.

So they were trapped. On a hidden, uncharted island. For who knew how long. While Cleo and the Black Sword wreaked havoc on the world.

Great. Just great.

"Tamsyn told me there's a problem here. What else happened?"

The others exchanged glances again, which was getting annoying.

"Follow me," Rowan said. He started off in the direction of a big circle of trees. As they got closer

Arella realized there was something in the middle, a tree stump.

Someone was sitting on the tree stump. A girl with long red hair pulled back into a loose braid, and she had freckles on her cheekbones and across her nose. She wore no armor, but had a small leather warrior's uniform on. Two twin swords were in sheaths at her sides and she had a tool belt with two empty potions strung to the sides.

Arella gasped.

"Cleo! How is she here?" she asked.

"I have no idea. I guess she has split personalities. Ezra thinks that when her evil side took over, her good side was banished here with us."

Cleo was clutching her head and murmuring disturbing things.

"No please! Stop! That's…" Arella caught Cleo say.

"How do we help her?" Arella asked. She didn't wait for an answer. She launched herself forward and squeezed into the tree circle.

"Cleo. Stop yammering and wake up." She said, shaking her shoulders. But as she did, visions flooded her brain. Eradoa and the Black Sword destroying the real world. Everyone who tried to stop them was killed, and the planet was now a field of corpses.

Arella understood what Cleo was feeling. Knowing you were responsible for such terrible things was more than she could imagine.

She also caught a glimpse of her inner thoughts. How confused and wrecked she was on the inside. Her mother was billions of years old, the ancient enemy of the world. She was deeply distraught about giving in to her mother's silver words so easily.

"Let's go back." Rowan said. Arella caught up with him.

"We have to figure out how to get her out of there. I'm scared she's going to lose her mind."

"I know. I'll talk with Ezra tonight. He said he had some ideas."

"Okay. But I saw what's going on in the real world. Eradoa and her mother are destroying everything."

"What did we expect?" he said grimly. He shrugged it off, but Arella saw the extreme anger and fear in his eyes. He was holding it together for the sake of the team. If he broke down, everyone else might lose hope. He had to be strong for them.

Arella nodded half-heartedly and followed him back to the others, who had started a fire. She knew there was nothing they could do now. She also knew that saving Cleo would have to wait. And she also knew that by the time they got there, it was a near one hundred percent chance that everything had been obliterated.

Arella could only hope that they escaped from this hidden island and saved the world before there was no world left to save.

THE END

Made in the USA
Columbia, SC
12 June 2024